This Puffin book

belongs to

....

The author acknowledges that this book was written on the lands of the Kulin Nation. She pays her respects to Elders past, present and emerging, and extends her respects to all Aboriginal and Torres Strait Islander sovereign peoples.

Little Gem

ANNA ZOBEL

PUFFIN BOOKS

PUFFIN BOOKS

UK | USA | Canada | Ireland | Australia
India | New Zealand | South Africa | China

Penguin
Random House
Australia

Penguin Random House Australia is part of the Penguin Random House group of companies whose addresses can be found at global.penguinrandomhouse.com.

First published by Puffin Books, an imprint of
Penguin Random House Australia Pty Ltd, in 2021

Cover and internal illustrations by Anna Zobel
Cover design by Christa Moffitt, Christabella Designs
Internal design and typesetting by Midland Typesetters, Australia
Typeset in 16/25 pt Garamond

Printed and bound in Australia by Griffin Press, an accredited
ISO AS/NZS 14001 Environmental Management Systems printer

NATIONAL LIBRARY OF AUSTRALIA

A catalogue record for this book is available from the National Library of Australia

ISBN 978 1 76 089608 9 (Paperback)

Penguin Random House Australia uses papers that are natural and recyclable products, made from wood grown in sustainable forests. The logging and manufacture processes are expected to conform to the environmental regulations of the country of origin.

penguin.com.au

For Dad, my brilliant co-author.

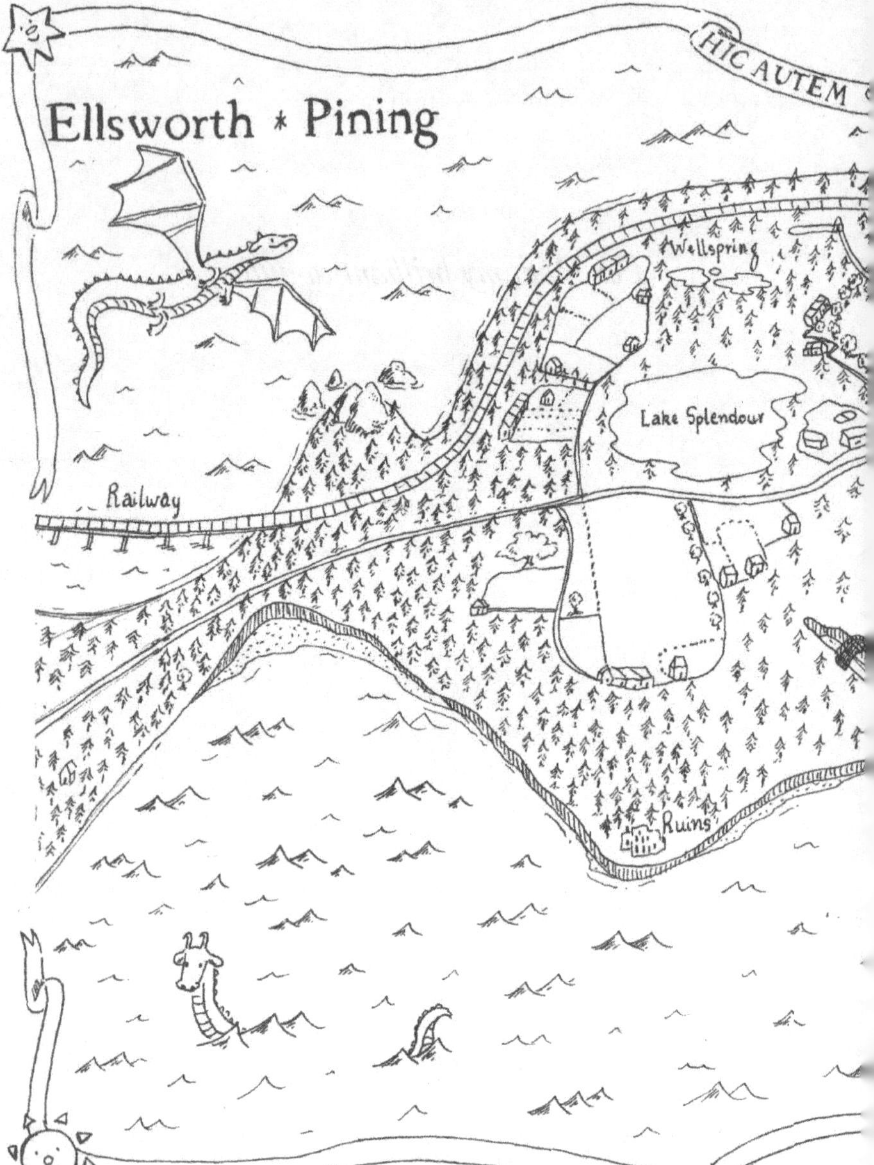
HIC AUTEM
Ellsworth * Pining
Wellspring
Lake Splendour
Railway
Ruins

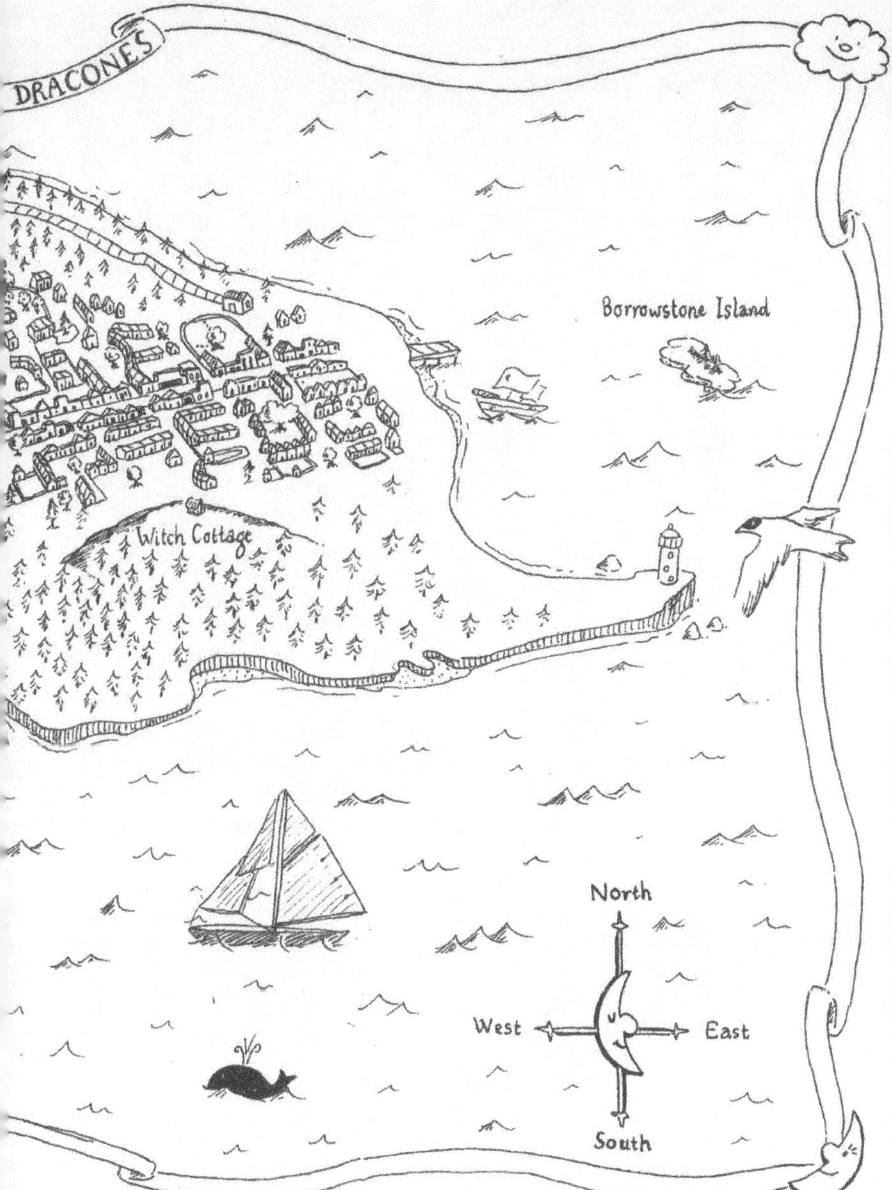
DRACONES
Borrowstone Island
Witch Cottage
North
West
East
South

Chapter One

There was a loud popping sound, followed by a heavy thump.

The kitchen had been silent and empty. Now a witch was sprawled across the floor. Her hat was crooked, and her long hair stuck out as if she'd been electrified. In one hand she was still holding a book of spells. The pages were smoking at the corners.

‘Oh!’ the witch cried out. She used her sleeves to pat the book until the smoking stopped. Then she stood up and looked around the room.

A moment earlier, Witch Gem had been at school, practising her travelling spells. But she did not seem to be at school any more. She was standing in a strange, empty house. Gem wiped at her knees, which were covered in dust and grime.

‘Where am I?’ she said.

Her voice echoed off the walls. The kitchen was small and cosy. There was a wood stove in the corner, just as dusty as the floor. The stone sink was green with mildew. Old pots and pans hung from hooks on the walls. Spiders hurried along the ceiling beams, and the windows were covered with cobwebs. Gem could see that the cottage had been empty for a long time.

She placed her spell book carefully on the dirty dining table, checking for smoke. Her travelling spell must have gone wrong somehow, Gem realised. She had only meant to magic herself from one classroom to another.

Maybe she had magicked herself to the caretaker's cottage, or to a house in the next town. Gem decided to open the front door and find out exactly where she was.

The iron latch on the door looked heavy and stiff. Gem tugged her patched hat down tightly over her head and rolled up the sleeves of her smock, which was far too large. Being short, she had to stand on the tips of her toes. The small witch pulled and pulled, using all her strength – and then the latch gave, and in a powder-burst of dust and dirt the door flew open.

Gem sneezed and rubbed her eyes.

It had been dark in the cottage, but outside the sun was shining. It was a beautiful spring day. The small stone cottage sat in a clearing on top of a hill. Behind the house was a forest of black pine and coastal she-oak. The garden had run wild. There were crowds of flowers of every kind and colour growing thickly together. Strong vines had grown over the walls, shading the windows, and the roof was covered in a blanket of moss.

Gazing down the hill, Gem could see the red rooftops of a small town. And beyond the town, to Gem's amazement,

lay the sea. It stretched bright and blue and glittering all the way to the horizon.

But Gem's school was on top of an icy mountain, surrounded by snow-covered peaks in every direction. It was nowhere near the sea. In fact, Gem had never seen the sea before.

'I'm afraid,' said Gem to herself, 'that my travelling spell has gone very, very wrong.'

Chapter Two

Witch Gem was used to having adventures. Many times she'd found herself on the wrong side of a spell. But magicking herself to a strange house on a strange hill in a strange town was a much bigger adventure than she had ever had before. She needed to find out where she was so that she could get back to school as soon as possible, before anyone noticed she was gone. 'My legs are short,' she told herself, 'and it is a long way, but if I don't start I won't finish.'

To get to town, Gem had to walk down a long flight of stone steps that ran higgledy-piggledy through the scrub and wild grasses. She thought about her calico cat as she climbed down. She'd last seen him curled up on top of a cupboard in the classroom, watching her sleepily. Poor Pomelo – she must have left him behind at school, all on his own.

The town came into view again. The little witch reached the bottom of the hill, out of breath. A wooden sign greeted her across the road. *Welcome to Ellsworth Pining,* it said in gold lettering. *Enjoy your stay!*

Gem had never heard of Ellsworth Pining, but she was sure that in town she'd learn where she was and how to get back to school.

Feeling confident, she stepped out into the road – but there was a sudden roaring sound. Before Gem knew what was happening an enormous red machine came speeding along the road towards her! Gem fell backwards. The rattling machine sped away as fast as it had come.

She stood up again slowly, her back muddy and her hair full of twigs. 'I'm not frightened,' she said out loud to nobody, once her heart had stopped pounding.

'I am definitely not frightened. But I will admit I am a bit confused.'

Gem followed the road until she reached the shops. Ellsworth Pining was a small town with one main street. The buildings, which had whitewashed walls and red-tiled rooftops, were packed closely together with little laneways in between.

It was the middle of the day and the street was very busy. When the townspeople saw Gem they gasped and smiled and whispered.

'A witch!' One girl pointed, pulling her mother's sleeve. 'Look, it's a real witch!'

Ignoring everybody, Gem hurried on. She would find out how to get home and then she would leave this strange place.

SHOE REPAIR
KEYS CUT
TOYS
TOYS
BEDSOR PHARMACY
SALE
IN STORE NOW
OPEN
SALE!
50%
50%
FORTUNES READ HERE
HAIRDRESSER
PHARMACY
SHOE REPAIR
MUST-SEE
OPEN 7 DAYS!

DENTIST
SPAGHETTI
COFFEE
GROCER
SANDWICHES
LOST:
SELLING

The main street was lined with tall, unusual lights. The first shop she saw had huge windows, much bigger than she had ever seen, and was full of colour: there were toy bears, and boxes of games, and even a model train that moved about. Next door was a pharmacy with a sign above the door that lit up all by itself.

The third shop was a barber, but what a barber! Women sat beneath strange round machines, chatting and reading. One man was having his hair blown about by a strange object with a long cord.

She reached a newsagency and stopped to look in the window. There were fishing magazines, boxes of coloured pencils and a stack of fresh newspapers with colour pictures.

NEWSAGENCY
50% OFF!
CROSSWORDS ON SALE NOW !!!!
100%
The ELLSWORTH PIPING Times SOLD HERE
MOVIE MADNESS
Hina Mito
AND
$
CLOTHES FOR COOL DUDES
elegance
STYLE

The witch looked at the date. It was still Thursday, but wait! She looked away, and then looked back again, squinting, her nose pressed up against the window. 'Surely not,' she cried out, surprising passers-by. 'Surely not!'

It couldn't be true.

Gem had tried to magic herself from one classroom to another, but instead she had magicked herself to a strange house. She had magicked herself to a strange town by the sea, far from everything she knew.

And she had magicked herself *one hundred years into the future.*

Her spell had gone very, very wrong indeed.

Chapter Three

Gem stood there, dazed, her nose rubbing the glass, for a long time. Her head was spinning. The future! How did she transport herself one hundred years into the future! Never before had her magic gone so wrong.

There was a screeching sound behind her. Gem turned to see that it was the same noisy red machine that had nearly run her

down on the road.

The wheels came to a stop, croaking gently, and two doors opened at the same time. A boy and a tall man got out.

'I told you I saw a witch!' said the boy breathlessly. 'Here she is again!'

Both of them were wearing a uniform of rough blue trousers and blue shirts with matching caps. The boy had a brown leather bag hanging over his shoulder.

'I'm Renzo,' said the boy, stepping forward

with his hand stretched out. His face was bright and friendly. 'This is my dad, Mr Donatello, he's the postman and I help him on school holidays. Sorry we nearly ran you over before – I guess you were walking down the hill from Witch Cottage. If we'd known a witch was moving in today we would have made sure the cottage was ready for you!'

Gem was surprised. She knew that all towns have a witch of their own. They are important in the same way that builders and doctors are important. They solve problems using spells and charms and potions, and communicate with the natural world in a way no one else can. A person might visit a witch, for example, if they had a wart that wouldn't go away. They might visit a witch if they needed good luck for a test, or their donkey was behaving strangely, or a gremlin wouldn't stop stealing socks from their washing line. Gem could tell, just by looking, that no witch had lived in Ellsworth Pining for many years. The town was lacking a dash of magic.

Gem adjusted her hat and shyly shook Renzo's hand. She had never met a boy before – there were only witches at Witchcraft School. 'I am the Witch Gem,' she said. 'And don't bother about the cottage. I won't be staying long.'

'Gem, is it?' said Mr Donatello with a smile. He had a thick moustache and bushy black eyebrows. 'Nice to meet you, Little Gem!'

'Not *Little* Gem, it's just Gem,' she said quickly.

But Mr Donatello didn't hear. 'Little Gem, you certainly are the youngest witch I've ever seen. We haven't had a witch in Ellsworth Pining for a long time. Not since . . .' He paused to think. 'Not since . . .'

'Since the Great Sausage Fire Incident,' Renzo reminded him.

'Ah. Yes. I won't be forgetting *that* in a hurry.' Mr Donatello coughed. 'Very unpleasant. Well,' he said, bowing slightly to Gem, 'it was terrific to meet you. A witch! Won't everybody be surprised! I'll see you again soon, I'm sure. Now I'd better keep delivering the mail before the engine gives out again – you know what these old trucks are like!'

'Oh, yes,' said Gem, who had never seen a truck before in her life. So that's what the red machine was called – a truck!

Gem turned back to the newsagency, wondering if they sold maps or time-travel potions. How could she travel back to her own time? The boy was still next to her. He looked very excited.

'Come on,' said Renzo, hopping from foot to foot. 'It's your first day here – I'd better show you around!'

Gem started to say no. Then she realised that a tour might help her after all. She might learn where she was, and how to get home. 'That sounds very nice,' said Gem. 'Thank you.'

Chapter  Four

'You have a funny way of speaking,' said Renzo as they walked around. 'Sort of old-fashioned. Is that how all witches speak?'

'Um – yes,' said Gem, hurrying to keep up with him. She wasn't ready to tell anybody that she'd travelled through time.

The boy himself spoke very quickly, in long, rambling sentences. His hands and feet were always moving. His energy reminded Gem of a wild rabbit.

Renzo showed Gem the main street, the train station and the pier. Everything was strange and modern. She saw more trucks, and electric lights, and fishing boats with noisy engines. At Witchcraft School, the buildings were built of heavy basalt stone, and the rooms were dark and gloomy. Here, many things were metal or glass, and there were so many lights! The world was certainly different one hundred years in the future.

It had been a big morning for Gem, and soon her legs were aching and her stomach was rumbling.

'I don't suppose we could find something to eat,' said Gem hopefully.

Renzo smiled. 'Come on, this way, Little Gem – I know a really great place.'

Renzo took her to Cafe Silva, which sat opposite the pier. The owner, Mrs Silva, was organising macarons in the display case. She was wearing a clean apron over a patterned dress, and her hair was pulled back into a neat bun. She had a round, friendly face.

When Mrs Silva finally noticed Gem, she stood up so fast she nearly banged her head on the counter. 'A witch!' she said with excitement. 'Oh my goodness! I'm Sara Silva, how delightful to meet you!'

'This is Little Gem,' said Renzo proudly. 'She's the new town witch! I'm showing her around Ellsworth Pining.'

PORTUGAL
the MAIDEN'S PROMISE
Hina Mito
SPECIALS
- vegetable stew
- creamy vegetable pie
- moussaka

'My name is just Gem, actually –' the witch began to say, but she was distracted by the sight of delicious food.

The interior of the cafe was brightly painted in green and white and pink. The tablecloths were embroidered, and the wooden chairs were padded with soft velvet cushions. There was a bookshelf in the corner, with a huge pile of *Movie Madness* magazines on top. The cafe smelt of butter and coffee and freshly baked bread, and the countertop was crammed full of the most delicious cakes Gem had ever seen. There were eclairs and tarts and lamingtons and fairy cakes and meringues and many more that Gem couldn't even name.

Gem and Renzo sat down at a table by the window and soon Mrs Silva carried a tray to their table. Gem's stomach rumbled. She hadn't eaten since breakfast, and travelling spells require a lot of energy.

'Lemonade for Renzo and tea for you, Little Gem,' said Mrs Silva, 'and some cream buns. I know witches have small appetites, but I do hope you'll try one.'

'I will admit I am partial to sweets,' said Gem, taking the smallest bun onto her plate. Mrs Silva sat down too, shaking crumbs from her apron.

Renzo reached into his satchel. 'I've got a letter here for you, Mrs Silva,' he said. 'My last delivery for the day.'

Mrs Silva took the white envelope and turned it over. 'Horrible handwriting . . . it must be from my brother, Emilio Dias.' She opened it carefully with a butter knife and pulled out a creased scrap of paper. There were just four words scrawled across it.

She read the letter aloud. '"*Special tip . . . orange replacement*," it says. What on earth can Emilio mean? Can you make any sense of this, Renzo?'

Renzo examined the paper, tilting it this way and that, before shaking his head vigorously. 'Makes no sense to me!'

Mrs Silva shrugged and tucked the scrap of paper into her pocket. 'My brother is the town Weather Worker,' she said to Gem. 'He'll be wanting to meet you. Why, we haven't had a witch here in a very long time!'

Chapter Five

'I suppose you've only just finished Witchcraft School!' Mrs Silva said.

'Um,' said Gem. As a matter of fact she had not finished Witchcraft School, but her mouth was full. The cream had been blended with strawberries, and the bun was so soft and buttery that it seemed to melt in her mouth.

'And I suppose you flew here on your

broomstick last night, and found Witch Cottage by yourself!'

'Um,' said Gem again, whose broomstick was far away and a hundred years in the past.

She took a second bun and crammed it into her mouth. She'd never tasted anything so nice in her life. The plate was empty now, but Gem wanted just one more. Quietly, she waved her hands under the table and muttered a spell. A new bun appeared on the plate with a *pop*, and Gem took it.

'Well, we're very glad to have you here,' said Renzo. 'I've always wanted to meet a witch – the last witch disappeared when I was just a baby. If you ever need anything, please ask me, I'd be happy to help.'

'As it happens,' Gem said, swallowing, 'I won't be staying too long. But this does seem like a very nice place.'

She heard a *pop*, and then another. Two more buns appeared on the plate. 'Stop now,' she whispered, waving her hands again. 'That's enough!'

Mrs Silva was nodding. 'You must be very talented, Little Gem, to have graduated from Witchcraft School at such a young age. No doubt they need a great witch like you in the big cities. But you know what they say, Renzo – when a new witch arrives in town, something mysterious is about to happen!'

'I doubt it,' said Renzo, drinking his lemonade. 'Nothing mysterious ever happens in Ellsworth Pining.'

There was more popping. Five buns, six buns, seven buns, eight – with a very loud *pop* a large bun appeared next to Renzo's foot.

'You're right, I'm sure, Renzo. Although the weather is very strange for spring,' said Mrs Silva thoughtfully, not noticing the buns popping up all over her cafe. 'It's been too hot, and too rainy. I wonder what Emilio is up to. It is hard work, controlling the weather all the time. I should visit him later.'

Gem was only half-listening but she did wonder what would happen if a town didn't have a Weather Worker. Witches were born with magic, but Weather Workers studied for many years to learn the magic they needed to keep the weather steady. They couldn't control all the weather, exactly, but they could push dangerous storms out to sea, or calm down wild winds. Without a Weather Worker in charge, the weather could go topsy-turvy.

Suddenly, a bun appeared on top of Mrs Silva's teacup. 'Why – where did all these buns come from?'

'There are two in my satchel!' said Renzo, looking in his bag.

Pop, pop, pop! There were buns on the counter, and the windowsill and in the flowerpot. Gem waved her hands furiously under the table.

'I suppose you were still hungry, Little Gem,' laughed Mrs Silva, standing up. 'Would you look at this? I'll have to call you when I'm tired of baking!'

'I do apologise,' said Gem, her cheeks red. She wiggled her fingers once more and the popping slowed down. There were cream buns all over the bakery.

'Well,' said Mrs Silva, still amused, 'I'll tidy this up, don't you worry. You'll need to get back to your witch business, Little Gem!'

'Of course,' said Gem, sliding a bun into her pocket. She wondered what she'd do now. Perhaps she'd find a map at the train station, or borrow an atlas from the library. She might find a clue in her spell book. But then Renzo intervened.

'That's right,' he said, finishing his lemonade with a slurp. 'You should be getting back to your cottage, Little Gem. Ghost Henry is probably awake by now.'

Chapter Six

It took Gem a long time to clamber back up the steps to Witch Cottage. The wind was strong and strange: it seemed to be blowing up, and then down, and she had to hold onto her hat the whole way. By the time she reached the top of the hill, the sun was low behind the forest.

And something else was different. Witch Cottage was not as quiet as it had been a few hours ago. Gem crept forward slowly. The front door was wide open, and every few seconds a cloud of dust burst through the doorway.

'Hello?' said Gem. 'Who's there?' She peered around the corner and inside she saw something very unusual. A small ghost, even shorter than Gem, was fiercely sweeping the floors of the cottage.

He was wearing an old-fashioned leather vest, pantaloons and a puffy-sleeved shirt. His shiny hair was cut into a bowl shape, and Gem noticed that he had one small green earring that sparkled in the light. Even in Gem's time, one hundred years ago, nobody dressed like that. Gem thought he must be a very old ghost.

'If I'd known a new witch was coming to Ellsworth Pining today,' the ghost was muttering, 'I would have had this cottage clean days ago! But no – nobody thought to wake up Ghost Henry, the witch housekeeper, all alone on the hill . . . I had

to hear it from the birds . . . all gossiping about it . . .'

He swept again and a fresh cloud of dust burst forth, covering Gem from head to toe. She sneezed into her sleeve and Henry noticed her for the first time.

'I suppose you expect me to apologise,' said Ghost Henry in a high, childish voice, 'but I didn't know you were coming! It's total chaos in here – and Witch Marisha left a huge mess behind after the sausage fire incident. It was her fault, after all, but still . . .'

He stopped and looked at Gem properly. 'You're young for a town witch, aren't you?'

'Yes,' said Gem, 'but don't worry. I won't be staying long. I do like your scarf, by the way.'

The ghost put down his broom and picked up a large wooden bucket, which he carried sternly past Gem into the front garden. He closed his eyes a little to show Gem he was angry. 'This isn't a *scarf*,' he said. 'It's a *ruff*, and, in fact, it was very expensive – it cost my parents six gold pieces and a prize chicken. It came all the way from Milan. Now, if you'll excuse me, I've got to hang out these blankets before the sun goes down or they'll never dry!'

Bubbles spilled out of the bucket and over his buckled shoes.

'I'm sure I know a spell for that,' said Gem helpfully.

She lifted her hands and chanted a magical spell. The blankets spun themselves in the soapy water, wrung themselves out and flew towards the washing line – but they didn't stop there. They flew upwards instead and draped themselves over the highest branches of the Tasmanian cedar tree in the corner of the garden.

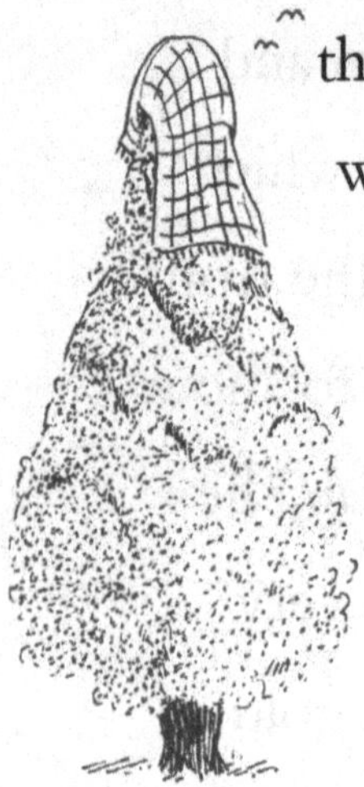

'Oh dear,' said Gem. 'I must have said the words wrong.'

'You really are very young. When exactly did you finish Witchcraft School?' said Ghost Henry, who went thin and wispy, so that Gem could see through him.

Gem didn't know what to say. Her whole body began to feel heavy and weak, as though she had the weight of the world on her shoulders.

'I give up,' said Gem, sinking down onto the doorstep and resting her forehead on her knees. It was no use pretending any more. This adventure was too big for one little witch. It was time to tell someone the truth.

Chapter Seven

'You see, Henry – I haven't finished Witchcraft School at all. I'm not even in my final year!'

Henry looked confused. He tipped out the dirty washing water underneath the hawthorn tree and then sat down beside her.

'How did you get here then?' he asked.

'This morning,' Gem explained, 'I was

at school, trying out my travelling spells. I had a test today, and – and I'm not good at travelling spells, so I thought I would practise. My teacher said that if I didn't do the spell correctly I'd have to scrub the school kitchen clean with my toothbrush, without using any magic at all, and last time it took me hours and hours. I was practising by myself and I only meant

to travel from one classroom to another. But instead I managed to travel here, to Ellsworth Pining – one hundred years in the future.'

'You *what*!' cried Henry. 'I'm over four hundred years old, and I've never met anyone who's travelled through time before!' For a moment he was so misty that Gem almost couldn't see him, but his voice was louder than ever.

'It's true,' said Gem sadly. 'I've no idea how to get back, and,' she went on, sniffing, 'I left my poor cat Pomelo behind, all by himself! I just know the headmaster will be furious! She's still cross about the time I turned the chimneys into drinking-straws – and the time before that, when

I melted all the socks. This isn't the first spell of mine that's gone wrong. I'm a very bad witch, really.' Gem's eyes filled with tears. 'A very bad witch indeed.'

Ghost Henry thought for a minute. Then he gave her a friendly pat on the shoulder.

'Well,' he said, growing solid again, 'I don't think there's much we can do about that today. Your cat will be fine, I'm sure, and you won't have to scrub anything with a toothbrush here. Let's finish our housework, and tomorrow we can look through the spell books and see what we can do.'

'All right,' said Gem, taking a deep breath. She pinched her cheeks and began to feel better. 'That sounds like a very good idea.'

Together they went back inside the cottage. They stood on chairs and brushed the dust and cobwebs from the ceiling.

Using her magic, Gem filled the sink with soapy hot water and washed all the pots and pans and plates. Together they mopped the rough flagstone floor until it gleamed.

Henry showed Gem to the loft bedroom upstairs. It was small, containing only an empty chest of drawers, a desk and a narrow brass-frame bed.

They cleaned the wooden floors and then they dragged the mattress outside and beat out the dust. Finally, Gem magicked the blanket down from the tree, where it had dried, and made the bed. She lay down on top of the patchwork quilt, her head against the pillow.

Through the window she could see the moon, and a small glittering light out at sea. Strange, rectangular clouds rolled across the sky.

'I'll just close my eyes for a moment,' she said.

It was a very comfortable bed, much nicer than her bed at school. The other witches were always sticking stones beneath her mattress or hiding frogs in her pillowcase. She began to worry about her poor, lonely cat, Pomelo, stuck at school by himself . . .

But she didn't worry for long, because soon she was fast asleep.

Chapter Eight

The next morning, Gem was woken by a loud knocking. She sat up with a start. Where was she? Why wasn't her bed cold and lumpy? Why weren't the blankets scratchy? The sun was up – she was supposed to be awake before sunrise! And where was Pomelo?

Then she remembered that she wasn't at Witchcraft School any more. She was in

Ellsworth Pining, far away from everything she knew. With a churning stomach, Gem pulled on her hat and hurried downstairs to answer the door. It was her new friend Renzo, satchel over his shoulder. He was very out of breath.

'Hello there, Renzo,' she said happily.

'Good morning! I've never had to deliver mail up here before,' he said. 'There are a lot of steps! I've got a parcel for you, Little Gem.' He held out a brown box tied up with string.

'Now I've got to keep making deliveries – see you later!'

'Thank you,' said Gem, wondering what the parcel could possibly be. Renzo waved and then he was gone, hurrying down the hill.

'A delivery?' said Henry. 'You've only been here one day!'

It was from Mrs Silva. Inside were some pastries, still warm from the oven, and a neat little envelope. Gem ripped the envelope open and read the letter aloud.

'Dear Little Gem,

Yesterday I mentioned that the weather was strange. You may have noticed the upside down wind and the unusual clouds. Well, after you left I went to check on my brother Emilio, the Weather Worker.

When I got to the lighthouse where he lives, I discovered that the door was unlocked, and my brother was gone!

Emilio would never leave the lighthouse without telling me. I am very worried. Can you help?

With thanks,

Mrs Silva

P.S. I hope you enjoy my apple-and-elderflower custard danishes.'

Gem put the letter down. 'I can't possibly help,' she said, her mouth full of pastry. 'I've got to figure out how to get back to Witchcraft School.'

But Henry looked excited. 'I'm beginning to think,' he said slowly, twisting his hair around one finger, 'that maybe you didn't magic yourself here by accident. Maybe you magicked yourself here for a reason.'

'What do you mean?' asked Gem.

'Maybe Ellsworth Pining needs you,' said Henry. He put the kettle on the stove and set out two teacups. 'Maybe you're not such a bad witch after all.'

The room grew dark. Gem glanced out the window and saw that the sun had been blocked out by a cloud shaped exactly like a saucepan. It turned into a shark shape before drifting away, and the room became light again.

‘I suppose that I could try to help. And then I can find out how to get back to school,’ said Gem reluctantly, examining the letter again. ‘It probably doesn’t make any difference if I’m gone for a day or a week.’

Except that poor Pomelo would be lonely, but she kept that thought to herself.

‘That’s the spirit,’ said Henry. ‘Now let’s have some tea, and then we can start investigating!’

Chapter Nine

Gem decided to go straight to the lighthouse. It was a warm day and she found that she didn't want to traipse down all those steps again. Gem looked at the old house broom in the corner. The paint was flaking off the handle, and the bristles were sticky with dust and cobwebs from yesterday's cleaning. It certainly didn't *look* like a flying broom.

Gem faced the broom and bowed. 'Please, old thing,' she said politely, 'can you fly?'

The broom was still.

'No,' said Gem, 'that's not right.' She bowed again, the tip of her hat scraping the floor. 'Please, oh wonderful broom, would you do me the honour of flying?'

This time, the broom twitched.

'Brooms do love compliments,' said Henry, washing the dishes, 'but that one hasn't flown for years and years. I doubt it can fly any more.'

At that, the broom jerked into the air and sped around the kitchen until it crashed into the cupboard and was still again.

‘There’s some life in it yet!’ said Gem, giving the broom a pat. ‘Come on, Henry!’

Henry turned around, his apron damp with washing water. ‘You want me to come with you?’ he asked, looking stunned. ‘Are you sure?’

‘Of course!’ said Gem. ‘Let’s go!’

Together Gem and Henry took the broom outside and climbed on. It shuddered and lurched as it rose up into the air.

‘I’m not sure about this,’ said Henry, holding on tight.

‘That way, please,’ said Gem cheerfully, pointing down the hill. It was a very slow broom, and it flew no faster than walking pace. ‘This is nice,’ said Gem, who didn’t like going fast anyway. 'Oh, look! That cloud is shaped like broccoli!'

'Yuck,' said Ghost Henry. 'When I was alive I hated broccoli.'

They flew past the town and towards the sea. People weren't used to the sight of a flying witch and a few stopped to wave and shout hello.

Gem and Henry skimmed over the treetops, and finally the lighthouse came into view.

'Over there, please, broom,' said Gem, pointing ahead.

As if it had misheard, the broom turned suddenly and tipped them both upside down into a gorse bush. Henry drifted down like a feather on the wind. Gem fell like a stone.

'No manners at all,' said Henry, dusting petals from the brim of Gem's hat. 'Well, I suppose we're walking from here!'

Gem picked up the broom. They would continue without magic.

It was a sunny morning, but it was raining in bursts out at sea. The lighthouse had been built at the furthest point on a narrow stretch of cliff, surrounded by sea on three sides. Below them, the waves crashed loudly against the cliff's edge, and the sea wind nearly blew Gem's hat away. Colonies of puffins waddled along the rocks, and above them a flock of terns swooped and dipped on the wind.

Gem felt happy. At school they didn't go outside very often. The surrounding mountains meant that they rarely got a glimpse of sunshine, and it snowed for half the year. The students spent all their time in the dark, damp halls, writing out spells into their copybooks. Gem was always spilling the ink, or getting her spelling wrong. She was in detention nearly every night. Ellsworth Pining was much nicer than school.

As they walked along the cliff, Henry suddenly paused. His eyes went wide. 'Can you hear that?' he said, turning wispy.

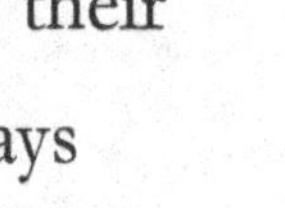

Gem stopped and listened. 'I can hear a gull screeching, I think,' said Gem. 'Is that what you mean?'

'I thought I could hear . . . howling,' said Henry slowly. 'But I can't hear it now. It must have been the wind.'

Chapter Ten

Then they heard a shout. It was Renzo, running up behind them in his uniform.

'Hello, Little Gem!' he called. 'And you must be Ghost Henry. I've heard lots of stories about you.'

'I'm sure you have,' said Henry smugly, tossing his hair.

'Are you both going to the lighthouse?' asked Renzo.

Gem told Renzo all about the letter from Mrs Silva.

'I see,' Renzo said. 'That's a bit strange. I'm sure Professor Dias hasn't gone far, though – he's probably back by now! I have a *National Birdwatching Association Magazine* for him, it's my last delivery this morning. We can walk there together.'

The lighthouse was the tallest building Gem had ever seen. It was built of stone and painted bright white. There was a large carving of a dragon set into the stone wall beside the front door.

'There used to be dragons here in Ellsworth Pining, you see, Little Gem,' Renzo explained. 'Professor Dias loves them. He's always reading about them. He had that carving made when he became the town Weather Worker.'

The front door was closed but when Renzo tried the handle it opened immediately.

'Hello?' he called loudly.

There was no reply. Inside it was dark and cool. There were old pieces of weather-magic equipment on the floor alongside piles of books.

'This way,' said Renzo. Gem and Henry followed him up a flight of twisting stairs. Through the windows Gem could see the sea foaming below them.

The stairs opened up into a cold, round room. It was a small space, but Professor Dias had made the most of it.

There were maps pinned to the walls, alongside charts showing the tides and the cycle of the moon. Above the kitchen bench was a poster displaying different types of bird eggs. A stuffed gull sat on top of the filing cabinet next to a collection of nests, and there were vases all over the room full of dried grasses and branches. A bookcase curved along one wall, and next to the desk was a large telescope looking out through the bay window.

'Professor Dias knows a lot about the environment,' Renzo said, picking up an enormous shell and peering inside. 'He's learnt all about plants and animals – you can ask him anything and he'll know it.'

Renzo put the shell down, then tapped a globe with his finger. It spun rapidly around. 'He even knows about the planets. He's a very intelligent person. I borrow books from him all the time.'

They continued to look about the room. Nothing looked wrong, but at the same time Gem felt that it wasn't *right*, somehow. It was a feeling she couldn't explain, and so she said nothing. Everything seemed to be in order until Renzo stepped behind the kitchen bench.

'This is really odd. Look here, Little Gem!' he said.

The pantry door had been opened. 'Claw marks,' said Gem, bending down to touch the wood. Some of the boxes had been chewed. A bag of flour had been dragged out and ripped open. There were footprints in the flour spread across the floor, but they weren't ordinary footprints.

They were animal footprints.

Chapter Eleven

'Professor Dias doesn't have a pet,' said Renzo, swallowing nervously. 'And the animal that made these prints has big paws. It must be something really ferocious.'

Gem could tell that Renzo was worried. Gem felt worried too. What was a wild animal doing inside the lighthouse?

Gem spotted a few strands of white animal hair on the floor, and she put them in her pocket. 'Well, that's one clue,' she said carefully. 'Let's continue to search and see what else we can find.'

On the kitchen bench, Gem noticed a pickle sandwich on a plate. It must have been made yesterday or the day before, because the bread was dry and the pickle slices were sweaty and curling at the edges. Someone had taken just one bite and left the rest. Beside the sandwich was an open book, a half-full mug of coffee and a strange jug.

'What is that?' she asked.

'You've never seen an electric kettle before?' said Renzo.

'Of course she hasn't,' retorted Henry. 'She's –' He was about to say that Gem was from one hundred years in the past, but Gem glared at him, and he managed to stop himself just in time. 'She's not a fan of coffee!'

'I see,' said Renzo, turning to examine the Weather Worker's desk.

Gem sighed with relief. There were so many new things in this modern world that she knew nothing about.

'I'm going to search all the rooms to be certain he isn't here,' said Henry, fading up through the ceiling.

Gem went over to help Renzo. There were weather-controlling tools on each side of the desk, but there was an obvious empty space in the middle.

'All Weather Workers keep a diary to keep track of the weather,' said Gem, looking around. 'I wonder where it is?'

'He does, and this is where he usually keeps it,' said Renzo, pointing to the empty space. 'He writes down absolutely everything. He's shown me before.'

'Where could the diary be?' said Gem. 'I'm sure it would have some clues inside.'

But they couldn't find it anywhere. The Weather Worker had hidden it – or taken it with him, wherever he had gone.

Henry reappeared. 'I didn't find anything,' he said.

'Professor Dias might have gone on holiday,' said Renzo hopefully.

TIDES

MOLLUSCS
DRAGONS

Gem frowned. 'Perhaps. Everyone is entitled to a holiday once in a while . . . but Mrs Silva said he never takes holidays. And I'm sure he would have found someone to look after the weather while he was away.'

They were about to leave when, glancing down, Gem noticed a wastepaper basket underneath the desk. It was empty except for a few torn pieces of paper.

'Look here,' she said, emptying the pieces onto the table. 'It must have been a map!' She could make out a grid and several handwritten markings.

'There are too many small pieces,' said Renzo. 'It probably isn't important anyway.'

'I think it probably is important,' said Gem, 'and even secret, if the Weather Worker ripped it up!'

‘It doesn’t matter either way, because it will be impossible to stick back together.’ Renzo moved towards the stairs.

‘I’m sure I know a spell for that,’ said Gem. She raised her hands and chanted a few words. The pieces floated up into the air and shuffled about until they formed a whole map.

‘Hooray!’ said Henry. ‘You’ve done a spell right at last!’

But he spoke too soon. As Gem reached out to touch it, the map burst into a small ball of flames. Ashes drifted slowly to the floor.

‘Oh dear,’ said Gem, feeling disappointed in herself. ‘I need to practise that one, I think.’

On the long walk back to town, Gem – still carrying her broom – thought about all they had seen at the lighthouse. The Weather Worker had clearly left very suddenly.

Too suddenly.

What had happened to make him disappear? And where was the lighthouse diary? What was the map for?

'Any ideas, Gem?' said Henry.

She shook her head. Her thoughts weren't clear yet. 'I'm too hungry to think,' she replied. Her stomach rumbled so loudly that a nearby pelican took off in fright. 'I think it's time we went back to Mrs Silva's.'

Chapter Twelve

Walking through town, Gem noticed something she hadn't before. There were dragons everywhere. The grocer's sign was decorated with dragons. There were dragon statues outside the library. Even Cafe Silva had two small dragons painted on either side of the door.

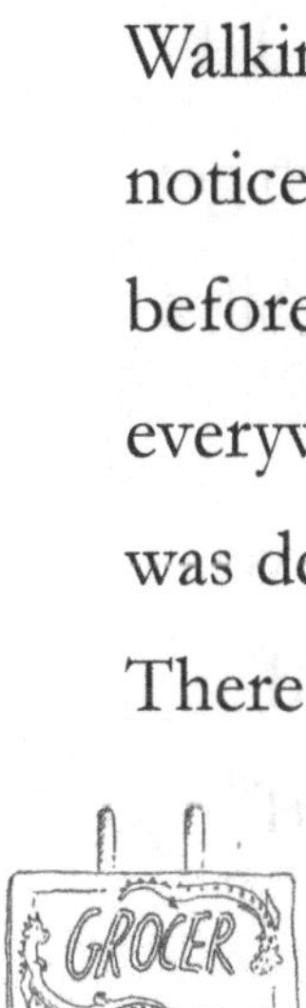

Gem had always been fascinated by dragons. Her favourite subject at school was Animal Magic. She wasn't interested in fairies or banshees or griffins: it was dragons she loved best. She loved to read stories about them protecting kind people, or going wild and burning down buildings with their fiery breath. Now she was in a town that seemed to like dragons as much as she did.

Gem, Henry and Renzo were glad to get to the cafe. It was warm and cosy. Mrs Silva was not behind the counter this time. Standing there instead was a girl, a few years older than Renzo, with a wide smile and bright, inquisitive eyes. A silky headscarf covered her hair, and her overalls were spotted with crumbs and flour.

'Hello, Renzo,' she said, leaning on the countertop with her elbows. 'Is this Ghost Henry? And this must be Little Gem! I'm Amira Von Zuhdi, I'm a waitress here.' She put a hand on her chest and smiled warmly. 'Lovely to meet you!'

'It's just Gem –' said the witch, but at that exact moment Mrs Silva came out from the kitchen.

'My, you all look hungry,' she said. 'Sit down, go on, and we'll bring you some lunch.'

A few minutes later Renzo and Gem were served hot pies on blue-patterned plates. Henry gazed mournfully at the table as the others ate, remembering the tasty pies he used to have on special occasions.

'Creamy vegetable today,' said Mrs Silva. 'Relish, anyone?'

The golden pastry was crispy on the outside, but soft on the inside. The filling, rich and cheesy, oozed out over their forks. Gem, who was used to eating cold mutton and hard-boiled turnips, finished hers faster than anyone.

'Did you get my letter, Little Gem?' asked Mrs Silva. 'I know you're very busy, but I was hoping you could help.'

'I did receive your letter, Mrs Silva, and thank you kindly for the danishes. We've already visited the lighthouse.'

'And?' said Mrs Silva anxiously.

'Your brother certainly wasn't there,' Gem said. Now that her belly was full she could think more clearly. 'It's obvious to me that he left the lighthouse in a hurry.'

'I see,' said Mrs Silva, 'but my goodness, I've just remembered – you shouldn't have gone to the lighthouse by yourselves!' Her voice went squeaky.

'Why ever not?' asked Henry.

‘Haven’t you heard?’ Amira called from behind the counter as she folded napkins. ‘Some of the townspeople are saying they’ve seen a vicious and horrifying beast on the cliffs, with huge teeth and enormous claws!’ She bared her teeth and pretended to scratch the air.

‘A beast!’ cried Renzo.

He, Gem and Henry all looked at one another. It must have been the beast that made those paw prints in the flour.

‘There’s no need to scare them,’ Mrs Silva scolded. ‘Nobody mentioned claws or teeth. Your imagination always goes wild when you’re thinking about animals, Amira! But people have heard howling, and some of the fishermen spotted something on the cliffs, so please be careful.'

'Mrs Silva,' said Gem, 'we did see animal footprints at the lighthouse.'

Mrs Silva went very pale.

'And I heard howling!' added Henry, who slowly faded and disappeared, sinking through the seat of his chair.

'Oh no!' Mrs Silva closed her eyes. Amira came over and stood behind Mrs Silva, rubbing her shoulders. 'Whatever can have happened to him?'

'Renzo said that your brother has a strong interest in flora and fauna,' said Gem. 'Is it possible he followed the beast to learn more about it? Or tried to catch it?'

'Yes.' Mrs Silva looked at Gem directly. 'Yes, that's certainly possible . . . my silly brother.'

'Please, will you help us find him, Little Gem?' said Amira.

Gem felt her fingers tingle with nerves. She had never solved a mystery before, but she couldn't let these people down. 'Of course,' she said. 'I shall do my best.'

Back at the cottage, Gem sat by the fire reading all the spell books she could find on the shelves. She was still reading many hours later.

'What next, Witch Gem?' asked Henry, handing her a cup of tea.

'We need to find the Weather Worker, and this beast, before anything bad happens,' said Gem, yawning. 'I think we need to solve this with a dash of magic. But first I need a good night's sleep!'

Chapter Thirteen

The next morning, Gem was woken by a familiar sound. She reached out to pat her cat Pomelo before remembering that he wasn't there. She realised that the sound was a howling wind blowing about the cottage.

She got dressed and went to find Henry but he wasn't anywhere in the house. Finally, she found him outside. He was

working on the roof with a pointed trowel and a bucket full of mortar.

'Did the wind keep you awake last night?' he called. 'It was so strong it blew some of the bricks loose from the chimney. This weather keeps getting worse and worse. If it keeps up, we could be in for a terrible storm.'

Gem looked down the hill towards the sea. The sky was blue with patches of dark, purplish cloud, and the wind blew the trees almost sideways. Leaves scattered through the air.

Gem considered the Weather Worker. He had disappeared in such strange circumstances – the door unlocked, a half-full cup of coffee left on the bench, as if he'd been having breakfast and then vanished into thin air. She needed to find him before this weather got any worse.

Henry finished repairing the chimney and floated down with his bucket and trowel. 'It's Saturday,' he said. 'That means crepes for breakfast!'

Gem had never had crepes before. Henry flipped the thin pancakes expertly in the griddle pan. He served them with melted cheese and chopped spinach.

Gem thought aloud as she ate her delicious breakfast.

'The first clue we have is the beast,' she said with her mouth full. 'We need to find it, and then maybe we'll find the

Weather Worker. I studied Animal Magic at school. I think I can remember a good spell for animal tracking.'

'That's a good place to start!' said Henry, still flipping crepes.

She flicked through her book until she came to the right page.

After Gem had washed her hands and face, she cleared a space on the dining table. She propped up her spell book so that she could see it clearly. Then she reached into her pocket and pulled out the white animal hairs she'd found at the lighthouse.

'I need a candle,' she said.

Henry took a candle from above the fireplace and lit it with a match.

'Perfect.' Gem began to wave the candle above the animal hair. She hoped with all her heart that the magic would work. She chanted the spell and watched with excitement as the hairs began to fizz and sparkle and bubble until they transformed into a small cold flame, hovering above the table like a firefly.

Then, with a small *pop*, the flame disappeared.

'Oh,' said Gem, looking upset, but Henry was already pointing out the front door. 'There, Gem, quick! You have to follow it!'

Gem and Henry raced outside. The flame was there, waiting for them. Then it disappeared again and popped up further along the garden path towards the steps.

'It's taking us to the beast!' said Gem. She felt very happy that her magic was working. She wanted to prove to Henry that she could do a spell right after all.

They followed the flame all the way down the hill. It seemed to be teasing them: sometimes they couldn't find it for a few minutes, but then it would pop up again, from behind a bush or a fence. At the road, the flame turned away from town and headed in the other direction.

'That seems right,' said Henry. 'It's taking us back to the lighthouse.'

Gem was out of breath but she kept hurrying. It was a cloudy day and the trees loomed tall above them, overhanging the road. The flame was bright and visible. It was steady despite the gusts of wind circling round them as it bounced along the road, appearing and then disappearing.

They had followed the dancing flame for nearly ten minutes when suddenly it veered off into the trees.

Gem saw the flame light up between the twisted trunks of two coastal oak trees before disappearing again. There was nothing else for it: Gem and Henry followed the flame into the woods.

The trees seemed to twist over and around them. The undergrowth was thick with dry bracken and sticky ferns. The canopy was so dense above them that they could no longer see the sun. Gem could

still see the flame but it was far out of reach, mocking them.

'I can't keep going,' said Gem abruptly. She had reached the edge of a deep creek. 'I don't know how to swim, and there's no safe way across!'

Henry floated ahead, completely unruffled.

'Could you keep going by yourself?' she asked.

'No,' said Henry indignantly, 'not without you! How would I catch the beast, anyway?'

Henry was right. Gem pulled herself out of the bracken and made her way back to the road. There was a rip in one of her socks and her shoes were filthy.

'The spell did work, at least,' said Henry, comforting her. 'We'll just have to try something else.'

'Yes,' said Gem, 'I suppose we will.' And they slowly began to walk back to Witch Cottage.

Chapter Fourteen

It was very peaceful at Witch Cottage. All Gem could hear was the singing of magpies in the cedar tree, and the wind as it gusted gently through the garden.

Gem browsed her spell book. She needed a new spell. A spell that would find the Weather Worker *and* the beast.

'At last!' she cried, leaping up and running into the garden with the book under her arm. 'Here's a finding spell that will work perfectly – much better than the tracking spell.'

'Pardon?' Henry peered over a lavender bush, holding his pruning shears. 'What are you shouting about?'

'I've got the perfect spell,' said Gem breathlessly. 'A finding spell, to find the Weather Worker. Is there any witch-hazel growing in the garden?'

'Of course,' said Henry, pointing to a flowering tree behind the kitchen. 'This is a witch's garden, remember!'

'Well, how about golden wattle? And billy buttons?'

'Just tell me what you need,' said Henry,

'and I'll show you.' Together they collected seventeen branches and stems of yellow flowers. The wattle made Gem's nose itch.

'All right,' she said happily, looking at the spell book, 'let's get on with it.' She was going to get this spell right!

Gem took a branch from the woodpile and drew a large circle in the dirt. Then she arranged the flowers and branches just like the picture in the spell book.

'This looks interesting,' said Henry. 'I've never seen a finding spell like this before.'

'Hush,' said Gem. 'I'm concentrating.' She took the final billy button in her hand and waved it above her head, chanting the spell. The circle of flowers rose up and began to spin.

‘It’s working!’ said Henry. Wattle fluff filled the air and the wind sped around them.

‘I did it,’ said Gem with excitement. ‘It’s going right!’

The air was tingling with magic. Gem wondered if the Weather Worker would appear in front of them! She realised she had no idea what the spell was going to do. She had never tried a finding spell before.

Gem heard an unusual clattering noise coming from the direction of town.

‘That must be the magic!’ she said, dancing from one foot to another.

‘Something is definitely happening!’ said Henry, pointing into the sky. ‘But it could be the strange weather.’

A low, dark cloud was flying towards them.

'It doesn't look right somehow,' said Gem uncertainly, magic still spinning around her. The cloud got closer and closer, and the jangling noise grew louder and louder.

'It's not a cloud at all, Gem!' shouted Henry, the wind ruffling his perfect hair. 'Look at that. It's – it's *things*!'

Shoes and jewellery and keys began to rain down into

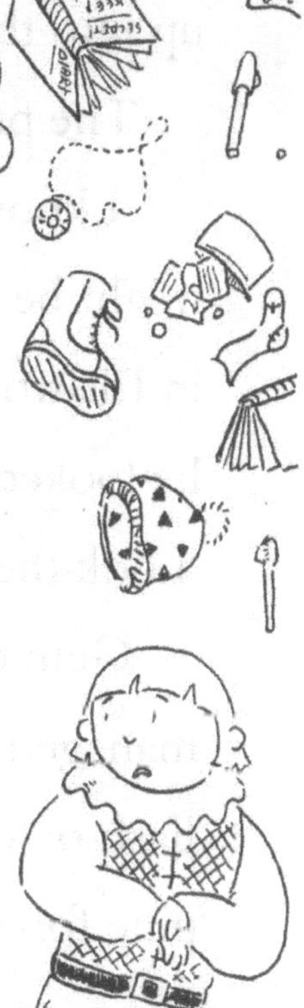

the dirt circle. Gem raised her arms to protect herself. She could see diaries and pencils and letters falling from the sky. There were modern items she'd never seen before – shiny tools and tiny machines and lots of things made of glass and metal – and they just kept coming!

Boxes thumped to the ground. Stuffed toys jostled for space with fishing rods and hammers and screwdrivers.

The clattering of objects made a tremendous din that sent crows cawing up into the sky.

The pile was taller than Gem.

'I know what's happened. I think this might be everything that's ever been lost in Ellsworth Pining,' shouted Henry. Then he looked over Gem's shoulder in shock. 'Look there, Gem. I think there's *a beast*!'

Gem quickly looked behind her. All she managed to see through the chaos was a flash of orange and white running into the pine forest. Could that be the beast? But in a moment, the beast, or whatever it was, had vanished into the woods. Gem didn't have time to see it clearly, let alone try a catching spell.

The rain of objects started to slow down. 'It's stopping, I think,' said Gem. But she spoke too soon.

There was a distant roar. Even from the hill they could see something dark and dripping rising out of the sea.

'Look out!' shouted Henry, turning see-through.

Gem ran for cover just in time. From underneath a tree Gem and Henry watched a rotting, slimy fishing boat speed through the sky and land in the garden with an enormous crash.

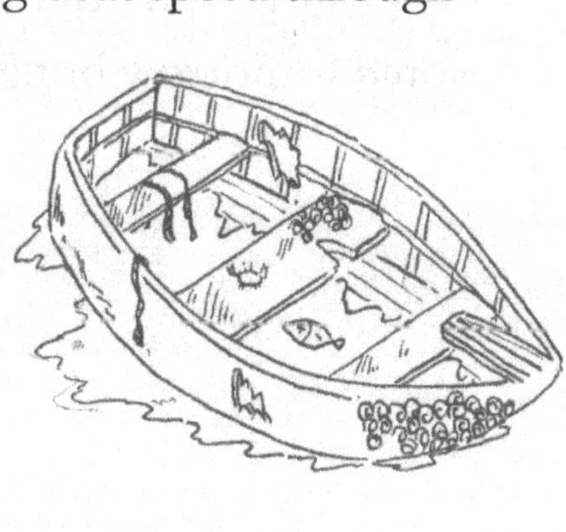

That seemed to be all. The air went still.

'I think that's Mrs Moridi's rowing boat,' said Henry. He had gone completely invisible. 'It went missing during the hundred-year flood.'

'I don't see any Weather Workers here,' said Gem, walking around the pile. 'I don't see anything useful at all.'

Her heart sank. They'd seen a flash of a beast, and then it had gone.

She was a hopeless witch. Why couldn't she do anything right? What disasters would tomorrow bring?

Chapter Fifteen

Feeling utterly miserable, Gem left the pile of things in the garden and crawled into her bed. She pulled the covers over her head and cried.

All Gem wanted was to be a good witch who helped people, but every time she tried a spell it went wrong somehow.

Gem felt as though she'd been born a bad witch. She'd never become a good witch, no matter how hard she tried. Her teachers were right: Gem was a hopeless case. She didn't belong in Ellsworth Pining, a town full of kind people who needed her help.

And she felt that she didn't belong in Witchcraft School either, even though she had lived at the school since she was a baby.

At Witchcraft School, classes ran every day except Sundays, from eight in

the morning until six in the evening, with homework every night.

The school was always cold and damp. On most days a fierce wind ripped through the mountain peaks and blasted any trees that tried to grow. If you were outside for longer than ten minutes without a scarf, your nose would start to freeze. It wasn't much better inside because it was so hard to get firewood up the mountains.

At Witchcraft School, you could be sent to detention if your shoelaces were untied, or your bed was unmade, or you held your pencil the wrong way, or wore your hat crooked – there were hundreds of ways to get into trouble. Gem had managed most of them, entirely by accident. The other witches always teased her for being so clumsy.

That night, Gem fell asleep thinking that she didn't belong anywhere at all.

When she woke up the next morning, Gem's eyelids were swollen from crying.

'Good morning,' said Ghost Henry, floating at the end of her bed with a cup of tea. 'This is for you. Time to get up!'

'I can't,' said Gem pitifully, curling up tightly under her quilt. 'I can't possibly get up. I need to stay here where I can't cause any more trouble.'

'Listen.' Henry put the tea down on her dresser and crossed his arms. 'Who magicked all those things into our garden?'

'Me.' Gem's voice was muffled.

'Whose job is it to magic it all away again?'

There was a long pause. 'Me,' said Gem with a sigh.

'Precisely. Now, hop out of bed and let's sort this out before we keep looking for the Weather Worker!'

Reluctantly, Gem came downstairs and found a returning spell in her spell book that she had tried at school. All she had to do was chant a few words over each object, and it would rise up into the air and zoom home to its rightful owner. They began with the old boat, and then they started on the smaller things – lost watches and teacups and wedding rings.

‘They’re probably all going into the ocean,’ said Gem glumly, watching a large leather boot speed through the sky towards town.

‘Cheer up,’ said Henry. ‘We’re working hard, and the pile is getting smaller!’

And it was. After a few hours the pile was only as high as their ankles.

‘Oh!’ said Henry suddenly. He bent down and reached into the small pile, pulling out a long chain. It was a necklace with a circular green charm. At one time it must have been gold but the metal had rusted to a dark brown.

‘What is that?’ asked Gem.

‘It’s a necklace I dropped into Lake Splendour when I was nine,’ he said,

giving Gem a funny look. 'No one was ever able to get it back out again.' He turned away and took it inside, staring at the green stone.

When he came back outside, they kept working. Finally, there were only a few things scattered in the dirt. Gem levitated a book into the air.

'Hang on,' said Henry. 'Don't send that one away. That says *Lighthouse Diary* on it!'

Gem took the book in her hands. Henry was right! It was the Weather Worker's diary, the one that had been missing from his desk.

They sat down in the garden and opened it. Today was Monday: nothing had been written since the previous Wednesday, when the Weather Worker had disappeared.

Last Monday, she read, it had rained heavily, and the Weather Worker had seen a pod of humpback whales. On Tuesday, he had used his weather magic to stop a terrible storm from coming to Ellsworth Pining, sending it out to sea instead. On Wednesday Amira had visited the Weather Worker at the lighthouse – and then the entries stopped.

Gem and Henry looked at each other with raised eyebrows.

'Amira!' said Henry breathlessly.

'If she was there the day the Weather Worker disappeared, then she must know something,' said Gem, her cheeks glowing with excitement. 'That's our next clue!'

Gem took the lighthouse diary inside and put it carefully on the dining table. Something had gone right after all. She'd done a finding spell, and she'd found every lost thing in Ellsworth Pining, including a clue for her investigation. That made her feel a little better. Gem finished sending the lost things home with renewed energy.

Their next task was to talk to Amira. Maybe the Weather Worker had told her where he was going and why!

Chapter Sixteen

Gem and Henry were about to fly into town when they heard someone huffing and puffing up the hillside steps. It was Renzo, carrying so many packages that he couldn't stand up straight.

'What on earth is this!' said Henry, putting down the broom. 'Is it your birthday, Gem?'

'No,' she said. 'At least, I don't think so.' She didn't know when her birthday was.

Renzo dropped the packages onto the grass. He removed his cap and wiped the sweat from his forehead. He was breathing very hard. 'Everyone in town is so grateful, Little Gem! That was very kind of you, to find our lost things and return them.'

'Oh,' said Gem, feeling surprised.

'I've got so many gifts here – Mr Tiatia has sent you a dozen pears from his garden . . . there's a basket of eggs – quail eggs, I believe. Come and look!'

Gem examined the packages in wonder. The train driver had sent two free train tickets. The dressmaker had sent a pair of soft satin pyjamas. There was a basket of blackberry

muffins from the pharmacist, Ms Bedsor, with a note attached:

Thank you for returning my favourite pen, I thought it was lost forever!

'How did they know it was me?' asked Gem.

'Don't be silly,' said Renzo. 'Who else would it be? You're the only witch in town!'

There were more notes. Josie the lawyer wrote:

Thanks for the jewellery case, Little Gem, but I think it must belong to Joyce, the labourer. I'll give it to her when she comes by. Thank you!

Moritz from the post office had received a camera (whatever a camera might be) that he thought belonged to

Maureen at the police station. Mr Lo had Ms Lough's car keys. George O'Conal was going to take Georgia Connell's hat to her carpentry shop.

'Of course some of them went to the wrong people,' said Gem, feeling disappointed. 'I'm useless!'

'Only some of them. Everyone is saying how clever you are, Little Gem,' said Renzo admiringly. 'It must have been a powerful spell!'

'It certainly was powerful,' said Henry. 'She magicked a lost necklace out of Lake Splendour, and a whole boat out of the ocean!'

Renzo was impressed. 'I think you are very kind, Witch Gem,' he said.

'You returned the lost things out of the goodness of your heart.'

Gem blushed. Renzo didn't know it had been an accident, and she didn't want to tell him. She didn't want anyone in town to know what a terrible witch she really was.

After quickly eating too many muffins, Gem and Henry flew into town on the old house broom. They urgently needed to talk to Amira.

The wind had grown even stronger, and it was a bumpy flight. The birds around them were tossed through the air, squawking madly as they flew inland, and Gem knew what that meant: bad weather was on the way.

'Looks like a storm is brewing,' said Henry nervously. 'We'd better find the Weather Worker soon, or we could be in trouble!'

Chapter Seventeen

They arrived at Cafe Silva but Amira wasn't there.

'She's away with her parents,' explained Mrs Silva, putting the 'closed' sign in the window. 'The whole family are volunteering at a wildlife rescue centre in Murble. They go there every year. She should be home tomorrow. I'm glad you're both here, though –

I wanted to warn you about the beast!'

'What about the beast?' asked Gem.

'Yesterday people heard it howling in town. A horrible howl, apparently.' Mrs Silva shivered. 'And you'll never believe it, but the librarian swears he saw the beast flying through the air! He said the beast was hairy and scary and monstrous, with enormous talons and a lashing tail.'

Henry faded and turned wispy. 'We thought we saw a beast near Witch Cottage yesterday,' he told Mrs Silva, 'but it ran off. We didn't get a good look.'

Gem remembered the flash of orange and white she'd seen

dashing into the forest. Could that really have been the beast?

'Just promise me you'll be careful,' said Mrs Silva. 'It's probably vicious. We have no idea where it could have come from, but I'm beginning to really believe . . .' Mrs Silva sniffled. 'I'm beginning to believe that my brother Emilio was attacked by this beast. Maybe even eaten!'

Gem was also worried that the Weather Worker had been eaten by the beast, but she didn't want to make Mrs Silva feel worse. 'We'll find him soon,' she said.

'When Arthur Tulip-Maidenport was kidnapped by a gremlin,' added Henry cheerfully, 'they found him almost straightaway. He was in a cave on

Borrowstone Island and all his clothes had been burnt to ashes. He lost four fingers to frostbite but otherwise he was all right!'

'Hush, Henry!' said Gem.

'I'm sure you're trying your best to find him,' said Mrs Silva. 'I'm just so worried about him, and I heard on the radio that an enormous storm is coming this way. A beast, a storm . . . it's all too much! I just –'

They were interrupted by a knock at the door. It was Renzo.

'Hello, Mrs Silva,' he said, stepping inside. Then he saw Gem and Henry. 'Oh, hello, you two! Sorry to disturb you, I can come back later.'

He went to leave but Mrs Silva stopped

him. 'Please come in, Renzo! Are you returning the book about dragons? Did you enjoy it?'

'Yes,' he said. 'It was really good! I finished it last night. Reading is the only thing that calms me down,' he explained to Gem and Henry.

'This is one of my brother's books,' said Mrs Silva. She showed it to Gem and Henry. 'He's crazy about dragons. You probably saw the dragon carving next to the lighthouse door. I keep this book in the cafe for anyone to read. You might be surprised to know that dragons used to live here, in Ellsworth Pining!'

'It's true, although I haven't seen one for at least three hundred years. Nasty creatures,' said Henry, wrinkling his nose. 'All that smoke!'

'Oh, I love them,' said Mrs Silva with a sigh. 'I wish I could see one. Apparently dragon eggs were large and blue. The dragons would lay them on Borrowstone Island. It took seven days and six nights for the egg to hatch.'

'Where's Borrowstone Island?' asked Gem.

'Out past the pier,' said Renzo. 'It takes about fifteen minutes to get there by boat.'

Mrs Silva sniffled again. 'If I wasn't so worried about Emilio I'd take you there for a picnic, Little Gem. It's a lovely place.

I'd bake a pie – make an apricot crumble . . . and Renzo, you could bring your camping stove to make tea, and your tarp in case it rains. But I'm simply too upset. When Emilio returns we can all go.'

'Professor Dias borrowed my camping equipment, actually,' said Renzo cheerfully. 'A few days ago. He took the camping stove and the tarp and everything. Maybe I should have told you. He said he'd have it back soon.'

'When did he borrow them?' asked Gem.

'I don't remember exactly. Last week, before you arrived?' Renzo shrugged. 'Anyway, I'd better go home.' He waved goodbye and headed out the door, satchel over his shoulder. 'See you soon!'

Chapter Eighteen

Gem and Henry flew back home to Witch Cottage. Gem was disappointed that Amira was out of town. She would have to wait until tomorrow to find out why Amira had visited Professor Dias the very day he'd disappeared.

The sun had vanished behind black clouds, and the wind was so powerful it nearly blew them into the branches of a huge elm tree. Gem had to hold tightly onto the brim of her hat so that it wouldn't blow away. Bad weather was brewing.

That evening Gem browsed her books for a long time but had no success. She had tried a tracking spell and a finding spell and wasn't sure what to try next. Gem fell asleep with her spell book open on her lap.

In the middle of the night, Gem was woken up by a loud thunderclap. The rain began to pour down, beating loudly against the roof. The room lit up with bursts of lightning.

Gem got out of bed and watched the spectacle from her window. She thought about her cat. Pomelo hated rain, and he was terrified of storms. He always hid under the bed when he heard thunder. Gem felt a bit scared herself, and she missed Pomelo very much. Shivering in her new silk pyjamas, she climbed back under the covers and pulled them up to her chin. Branches scratched against the windows and wind howled around the house. It took a long time for Gem to get back to sleep.

It felt as if she'd only been asleep for five minutes when Gem was woken again. She sat up with a start. It was morning, but the sky outside was dark with cloud. Ghost Henry was shaking her shoulder.

'I can hear that howling again!' he said urgently. 'I think there's a beast outside the cottage!'

Gem could barely see Henry in the dim light. He was floating above the floor, his outline shimmering in the dark. Gem got out of bed and put on her hat.

Now she could hear the howling too. It was distant but perfectly clear.

It was time for Gem to catch the beast.

But then Gem's knees began to shiver. Her stomach churned like a rolling barrel. She felt two opposite feelings at the same time – that she couldn't possibly capture a beast by herself, and that she *had* to capture the beast. She couldn't let the people of Ellsworth Pining down. They expected her to help them.

'Don't go, Gem!' said Henry. 'We can't do this by ourselves! Mrs Silva said the beast could fly – that it had enormous talons – and a lashing tail!'

But Gem was already pulling on her waterproof rubber boots and picking

up the house broom. 'I have to do this,' she said, trying to sound confident. 'I'm the town witch, for now at least, and it's my job to help. I have to try.'

Henry, see-through and misty, followed her into the rain. Everything was shadowy and grey. The sun was low in the sky somewhere, but it wasn't visible through the drizzle and cloud.

Gem turned to her left. A figure cloaked in black was coming slowly up the steps towards her. Gem's heart jolted – and then she realised it was Renzo wearing a black rain jacket!

'Little Gem!' said Renzo. 'I was just coming up to bring you this letter from Mrs Silva, but now I can hear howling! Are you all right?'

'It's the beast,' she said, her voice shaking slightly, 'and we're going to catch it.'

Renzo looked very serious. He put a hand on Gem's shoulder. 'I'm coming with you,' he said bravely. 'I'll walk through the forest.'

Gem got on her broom. 'And I'll see if I can spot the beast from the air,' she said, taking off.

Henry clung on behind her, barely visible. 'I don't like this, Gem,' he said, his voice quivering. 'I don't like this one bit.'

Chapter Nineteen

Rain ran down Gem's hat and dripped over her eyes. Her fingers felt frozen. The fierce wind knocked the broom about like an autumn leaf and drove the cold rain straight into her eyes. The trees were buried in cloud and mist. She could just make out the top of Renzo's head as he walked along below them. Gem clung onto the broom as tightly as she could and peered ahead, looking for any sign of the terrible beast.

Suddenly there was a shout from Renzo. 'I can hear it!' He pointed towards the cliffs. 'That way, Little Gem!'

The hunt was on. Gem flew just above the trees on her slow broom. The clouds and rain made everything blurry. She was so scared she felt like a snake was wriggling in her stomach.

'I can see something!' yelled Renzo again. He pointed to a tall black pine. 'There!'

Now Gem could see what Renzo had seen: a patch of orange and white, barely visible among the leaves and branches. She tilted the broom down towards the trees and flew as fast as she could, remembering a catching spell she had learnt at school.

The wind pushed her from side to side, scraping her shoulders and elbows against the tree trunks, but she held the broom steady and flew on.

The beast was on the lowest branches of the black pine. Quickly, Gem chanted the catching spell. There was a blaze of sparks and a net appeared in midair. In one swift movement it wrapped itself around the beast. The animal fell a short way from the branches and onto the ground, howling even louder than it had before.

'You did it!' Henry was amazed. 'You got the spell right!'

Gem landed her broom and crept closer to the net, wiping rain from her eyes. She had caught the beast all by herself! She had been brave – as brave as any good witch – and she had caught the beast!

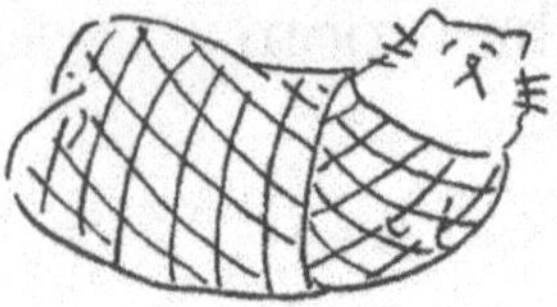

The creature wasn't as big as she had first thought. She could see no talons or wings or fierce sharp teeth. It was a straggly thing, orange and white and brown, with large sad eyes and very wet fur.

It wasn't a beast at all . . .

It was her cat, Pomelo!

Chapter Twenty

Gem pulled off the net and hugged Pomelo to her chest. She couldn't believe it. All this time she'd thought he was at Witchcraft School by himself, but he'd been here, in Ellsworth Pining, alone and hungry! He was very wet and very miserable. Gem held Pomelo tightly as he shivered in her arms.

'I'm sorry, Pomelo,' she said, with tears

in her eyes. 'I didn't know it was you. I thought it was a horrible beast!'

'What's going on?' said Renzo.

'I don't know how to explain it – you see, it's my cat.' Gem held Pomelo tightly. 'I thought I'd left him behind at school!'

She felt many feelings at once – joy, at finding her cat; sadness, that Pomelo had been alone for many days; and embarrassment, that she had thought he was a beast. She was sure that now Renzo and Henry would realise what a bad witch she really was.

'So it's not a beast at all, then,' said Henry. 'It's a cat!' He sighed – but it wasn't a sigh of disappointment. It was a sigh of relief.

'This is *such* good news,' said Renzo. He stepped forward and gave Pomelo a scratch under the chin. 'That net spell you did was the best thing I've ever seen! What a relief we didn't have to capture an actual beast! I don't know what we would have done with it. I love cats. And this one can fly,' he went on dreamily. 'The librarian said he saw the beast flying, remember? But I suppose all witches' cats can fly!'

Witches' cats couldn't fly, but Gem was too overwhelmed to say anything.

'Well, I'd better keep going with the mail run – I wish I could stay,' said Renzo regretfully. 'Here's the letter I was going to deliver to you.' He passed Gem an envelope and she put it in her pocket. 'I'll see you later!'

And he was off, following the path out of the forest and down the hill.

'Come on, now,' said Henry, who had stayed beside Gem the whole time. 'I'll carry the broom. Let's get that cat home and warm him up!'

Back at Witch Cottage, Henry built a fire, and Gem rubbed Pomelo with a towel until he was dry. Gem gave Pomelo a look-over. He was not a small cat, but he had lost weight and his soft fur was dirty.

'Poor kitten,' she said, feeding him pieces of boiled chicken. 'You must have had a hard time in the wild all on your own.'

'I suppose that when you magicked yourself to Ellsworth Pining, you also magicked Pomelo here,' said Henry, 'and he got lost.'

'I suppose I did,' said Gem. 'Those must have been his footprints in the flour at the lighthouse! He was looking for food.'

'And when you accidentally magicked all the lost things in Ellsworth Pining to our garden, you brought Pomelo here too, because he was lost, but he ran off into thc forest. That's why the librarian saw him flying through the air! He's quite a big cat, isn't he? I'm surprised he can run so fast.'

‘He has big bones,’ said Gem lovingly. She was so happy to have Pomelo with her again! She had missed him very much. She scratched his ears and was pleased to hear him purr.

‘Let’s think about this,’ said Henry. ‘You did a finding spell, and all the lost things in Ellsworth Pining ended up in our garden.’

‘Yes . . .’ Gem kept scratching Pomelo.

‘Well,’ Henry continued, ‘what if the Weather Worker isn’t lost at all?’

Gem looked at Henry with interest.

‘What if he’s gone – on purpose? We know he hasn’t been eaten by a beast. He must be around Ellsworth Pining somewhere.’

‘That’s a very good point,’ said Gem.

The finding spell *had* worked after all – it just wasn't the right spell!

Then she remembered the letter in her pocket. It was from Mrs Silva.

'Dearest Little Gem,' she read aloud,

'I have been thinking about something all night. Yesterday Renzo said that Emilio borrowed his camping equipment. Why could that be? Do you think it means something?

Your friend,

Mrs Silva'

There was a short pause, and then Henry and Gem spoke at the exact same time.

'The Weather Worker has *gone camping*!'

Chapter 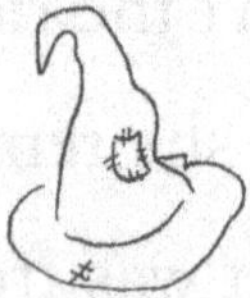 Twenty-one

Outside, the rain had slowed to a trickle. The sun shone down in beams through thick grey cloud. The weather seemed calm, but Gem could tell that it wouldn't last for long. Part of Gem wanted to stay with Pomelo all day in the cosy cottage – but at the same time, having Pomelo with her made Gem feel braver and stronger than before.

‘I know what we have to do,’ she said to Henry after a late breakfast. ‘Amira should be back today. We need to talk to her and find out what she knows.’

They set off straightaway. The garden was a maze of puddles, and raindrops sparkled along the tree trunks like tiny jewels.

As they flew towards Cafe Silva, they saw flooding in the lower parts of town. Seven spectacular rainbows hovered in the distance.

‘That was the end of the bad weather, hopefully,’ said Henry. ‘If it gets any worse we could be in real danger. Ellsworth Pining could end up underwater!’

The drains along the main street had

blocked during the storm. Shop owners were busy clearing the drains in case it rained again. Henry floated along beside Gem, who plodded through the ankle-deep water in her rubber boots.

There was a 'closed' sign hanging on the door of the cafe. That was unusual. Gem knocked anyway. When Amira opened the door, a gush of water poured out onto the street.

'Oh, thank goodness you're here, Little Gem,' said Amira, who had a streak of mud on her forehead. 'It's a disaster!'

Cafe Silva was completely flooded.

Amira, wearing waterproof fishing trousers and red rubber boots, was trying to mop the water out the back door, but it wasn't making any difference. And flooding wasn't the only problem: giant hailstones had smashed through the north-facing windows. The hailstones were still there, melting in the floodwater like tiny icebergs.

'I got back from my holiday last night and came straight here this morning after dawn prayers. Mrs Silva was so upset that I told her to go home and lie down,' said Amira despairingly. 'I've got no idea what to do by myself! It's even flooded in the kitchen. I was just about to go to Witch Cottage and ask for your help.'

'Well, we're here, and we can definitely help you, can't we, Gem?' said Henry, who was very proud of his housework skills.

'Of course,' she said firmly, looking at the windows. 'I'm sure I know a spell for that.' Taking a deep breath, Gem chanted a fixing spell. The glass fragments lifted up and joined back together in the window frames. She concentrated very hard – she didn't want them to burst into flames like the letter in the lighthouse.

'Fantastic,' said Amira. 'You really are amazing!'

But as they watched, the glass began to change.

'Oh dear,' said Henry. Some of the pieces turned yellow and others turned

green and purple and blue, until each window was a patchwork of colour.

'Why, you've coloured the glass for Mrs Silva!' Amira exclaimed. 'You know how much she loves colour!'

A ray of sunshine burst through the window, casting rainbows over the floodwater.

'Yes,' said Gem, grinning at Henry, 'that is exactly what I meant to do.'

Chapter Twenty-two

It took a long time to clean up the bakery. Gem's broom set about by itself, knocking the hailstones through the doorway with surprising strength. Water can be very tricky to move with magic, even for experienced witches, so Gem and Henry and Amira used buckets and mops instead. Finally, the water was gone and they could see the real damage. The water had made the walls muddy. The tables and chairs and tablecloths were wet. The kitchen cupboards were soaked, the flour ruined.

'We worked so hard and it still looks awful,' said Amira, leaning on the counter. 'Maybe we should just give up.'

But Gem was feeling tough.

'We can do this,' she said, pulling down her hat. 'We just need a dash of magic!'

While Henry and Amira scrubbed the walls and floors, Gem used heat spells to dry the furniture. The flour couldn't be saved, but by the end the cupboards were dry and clean.

'I'm sweating now,' said Amira happily. 'That heat spell is really working.'

'It seems to be going right,' said Henry. 'You are a good witch, Gem!'

It was finally done. It had taken them nearly four hours. The bakery was not the same as it had been: the rainbow windows sparkled, and the tables had burn marks here and there from the heat spell, but it was clean. Amira found some cinnamon custard scrolls that had escaped the floodwater, and they ate them sitting on the countertop.

'Thank you both so much for your help,' said Amira. 'I couldn't have done it without you.'

'That's all right,' said Gem. Now was the perfect time to ask Amira some questions. 'Amira, why were you at the Weather Worker's lighthouse last Wednesday?'

'How do you know about that?' Amira said with surprise.

'We found the lighthouse diary. It was lost.'

'Oh! Well, when I grow up I want to be a Weather Worker myself. I just love the outside world. I visit Professor Dias all the time, because he knows so much! He taught me about plant names, and moon cycles, and how to tell which bird is which.

He showed me how to tell when a storm is coming, and when to look for whales, and how the tides work. I've been so worried about him this last week.' She looked really upset. 'Are you any closer to finding him?'

'Yes, we've found a few more clues. And we know he wasn't eaten by a beast,' said Gem, glancing at Henry. 'Of that we're certain.'

'Thank goodness!' Amira put her hand on her heart.

'So when you visited him last Wednesday you were just there to talk about birds and moons?'

Amira thought for a moment. 'No. I was there to show him a rock I'd found. It was beautiful and smooth. I'd never seen anything like it. I brought it to Professor Dias and he had no idea what it was. He was going to look through his books to see if he could identify it.' Then Amira looked towards the door and stood up. 'Mrs Silva is back!'

Mrs Silva stepped inside the cafe. She was carrying buckets and mops, but she put them down and pulled all three of them into a tight hug. Henry half-faded through her arms, but joined in anyway.

'My goodness,' she said, weeping, 'I didn't expect this! I didn't expect this at all. My shop looks even more beautiful than it did before!'

Chapter Twenty-three

Gem told Mrs Silva all about finding her cat Pomelo in the woods. Mrs Silva wept with relief that her brother hadn't been eaten by a flying beast. By the time Gem and Henry headed home on the old house broom, it was drizzling again.

After dinner, the rain began to beat down, even harder than the night before.

ELLSWORTH
PIMUG

The thunder seemed to come every minute and the lightning was relentless. In front of a warming fire, Henry and Gem went through the clues again, with Pomelo curled up right by the flames.

'Emilio borrowed Renzo's camping equipment. Amira came to his house to show him an interesting rock on the day he disappeared. Afterwards, he made himself a sandwich and a pot of coffee – and then he vanished somewhere.'

Henry nodded. 'Now we just have to figure out how those pieces fit together. If the Weather Worker has gone camping, why didn't he tell anyone? He has a very important job, and we've had one dangerous storm after another. It must be out of character for him to abandon the town.'

'Exactly!' said Gem, eating her third pear.

A pink flash of lightning lit up the room, reflecting against the glass in the picture-frames.

'I'll be sorry when this mystery is over and you figure out how to go back to school,' said Henry. He floated down to the floor. 'I'm enjoying spending time with you.'

'You are?' said Gem. She felt surprised.

'Yes!' said Henry. 'The other witches never asked me what I thought, or took me anywhere. I stayed here in the cottage all the time, by myself, cleaning up spilt potions and dead beetles. Witch Marisha used to throw onions through me when she was unhappy, and the witch before her called me "misty servant"! I know I'm the housekeeper – that's my job and I enjoy it – but you have a big heart, Witch Gem. You're a special witch, and powerful too, even if you don't get your spells right all the time.'

Gem blushed. 'I like spending time with you too, Ghost Henry,' she said. 'Thank you for being so kind to me.'

She realised that Henry was her first real friend. Mrs Silva, Amira and Renzo had become her friends too. She understood, all of a sudden, that she felt happy. Gem couldn't remember ever feeling this happy before. At Witchcraft School she'd mostly felt scared, worried and lonely. Now that she had Pomelo with her in Ellsworth Pining, everything felt perfect.

'Maybe there'll be another mystery after this, Henry,' she said, opening a box of chocolates. 'You never know!'

For the first time, she found herself wondering if she really had to go back to school. Could she stay in Ellsworth Pining forever?

Chapter Twenty-four

The next morning, a bright ray of sunshine burst through the storm clouds and streamed through the bedroom window. A cloud shifted, and the light landed on Gem's sleeping face. Her eyes opened slowly, and then they opened wide.

'Aha!' she shouted, leaping out of bed. Pomelo fell off the covers in fright.

‘I’ve got it!’ she yelled, storming down the staircase. ‘I’ve got it, Henry!’

Henry looked up from his armchair, where he was busy darning socks. ‘What have you got?’ he said mildly. ‘Fleas?’

But Gem didn’t answer. ‘Come on,’ she said, grabbing the house broom and a ball of string. She had the Weather Worker’s lighthouse diary under one arm.

‘What on earth are we doing?’ asked Henry as Gem burst out into the garden and climbed on her broom.

‘I had an idea,’ said Gem, holding out the diary in front of her. ‘I was dreaming about flying books, and – just listen to this! I’m going to put a returning spell on the diary, just like we did with all the lost things, and we're going to follow it to the Weather Worker!'

The broom rose up into the air. 'Ooh,' said Henry, looking impressed. 'I like that. Very good thinking!'

'I know,' said Gem. 'Watch out, though, because it might be a bouncy ride!' Carefully, she tied the book to the broom, wrapping the string around the handle many times. Then Gem stared at the book, and with fierce concentration she chanted the returning spell.

The book shivered, as if waking up. It trembled. It shook – and then it shot into the air with surprising strength, dragging the broom along with it.

'Hold on!' shouted Henry.

Gem leant down and wrapped her arms around the handle. It was like riding an angry bull. Pulled along by the book, the broom jerked and twisted through the air, nearly throwing Gem and Henry to the ground.

'We're going . . . towards . . . the lighthouse,' said Gem through gritted teeth, reaching up to pull down her hat. It was true. The book was tugging them towards the Weather Worker's home.

The ride got bumpier over the trees. Gem screamed as the broom twisted upside down. It shot up into the air and then down again as the book struggled to get free.

'We're going down!' Henry shrieked,

completely invisible except for his hair. 'Watch out!'

The broom tore through the treetops, bumping roughly along.

'Ouch – ouch – ouch – ouch,' said Gem, scraped by branches.

A flock of birds burst out of the trees, screeching in fright.

The broom pulled up again suddenly, into the sky. Gem's hair was full of leaves and feathers. They were still heading towards the lighthouse – they just had to hold on!

Gem could tell the broom was tiring, but the book kept pulling. The book went up, and the broom hung vertically below. It took all of Gem's strength to hold on.

DIARY

The string started to loosen. 'No,' she shouted, leaning upward to grab the book – but she only managed to grab one page, which tore out, and with one final jerk the book tugged itself free and shot off through the sky.

The old house broom sank slowly into the treetops. Gem, tucking the torn page into her pocket, found her feet on one of

the branches and held on, watching the book vanish into the distance.

'It's not going to the lighthouse at all,' she said to Henry, brushing a caterpillar off her cheek. 'It's going out to sea.'

They both watched as the book flew past the cliffs and over the water until it was no longer visible.

'I suppose I did it wrong again,' said Gem, sighing. She felt disappointed with her great idea.

'You might have,' said Henry, trying to comfort her, 'or the Weather Worker is on a boat.'

'I doubt it,' said Gem, beginning the long climb down the tree.

But then Gem's eyes lit up. She opened her mouth and for a moment no noise came out.

'It – it – Henry, it was going out to sea!'

'Yes?'

Gem clapped her hands together. 'It was going towards Borrowstone Island!'

Chapter Twenty-five

The broom was exhausted, so they left it at the door of Witch Cottage and hurried on foot into town. They found Mrs Silva and Amira at the cafe. Renzo and his father were there too, drinking lemonade at the counter.

'Hello again, Little Gem –' said Mr Donatello, but Gem interrupted.

'He's camping, I think, on Borrowstone Island!' she said breathlessly.

Mrs Silva gasped. 'Emilio? Camping? Are you sure?'

'Yes!' said Gem. 'I mean – no, I'm not sure – but I think so.' She looked outside at the gathering clouds. 'Another storm's about to come – we should go now – but my broom is too tired!'

'Our boat,' said Renzo immediately, looking to his father. 'We can take you.'

'Not without me,' said Amira.

'And I'm coming too!' said Mrs Silva. She was already

taking off her apron and fetching her hat. 'If I find out that Emilio has caused me all this bother and worry just to go camping, I'm going to be furious!'

They strode across the road to the pier. It was Gem's first time in a boat. This one was red and shiny, like Mr Donatello's truck, with enough room for all of them

to sit comfortably. Mr Donatello powered up the motor and the sound gave Gem a shock.

There was no rain or wind. The air was still, but the clouds felt heavy and ominous. Another storm was brewing, and Gem knew this one would be even worse. Trees would fall. Buildings would be damaged. The streets would flood and people could be seriously hurt.

Gem knew they had to act quickly.

The boat went fast through the calm water. Soon Ellsworth Pining was far behind them and the only thing they could clearly see was the lighthouse, the automatic light flashing brightly against the dark sky. Borrowstone Island came

into view. It was rocky and mossy and covered in trees. Mr Donatello steered the boat towards a small pier.

'It's beautiful, isn't it, Little Gem?' said Amira, climbing out. 'Just beautiful!'

Small blue butterflies fluttered by their heads, and they could hear the hungry calls of nesting chicks in among the rocks. As they walked up the beach, Mr Donatello told them some of the history of Ellsworth Pining.

‘Hundreds of years ago, there were very few people here: a handful of farming families, and one wealthy family with a mansion on the western point.’

‘That was my family home,’ said Henry importantly. ‘It’s all ruins now, of course.’

‘It is,’ said Mr Donatello, ‘because a few hundred years ago the roof was burnt down by an angry dragon.’

‘Really!’ said Amira. ‘I had no idea! I would give anything to see a dragon.’

‘Dragons laid their eggs on this island and then the dragon mother breathed fire on the egg for a full week,’ Mrs Silva explained.

‘They need the heat or they can’t hatch,’ said Gem. ‘We studied them in Animal Magic.’

‘I can almost smell the smoke,’ said Amira dreamily. ‘Amazing creatures!’

‘You wouldn’t think so if a dragon burnt down your house,’ whispered Henry gruffly.

Gem looked over at Henry, her eyes suddenly sparkling.

Gem had another idea – and it was a good one.

Chapter Twenty-six

'Now where could my brother be?' said Mrs Silva impatiently.

All they could hear was the chirping of birds and the low hum of insects.

'Be careful of the nests, and don't step on any plants,' said Amira, leading them into the trees. 'We must be really quiet so we don't disturb the animals. This is a very special place!'

Renzo strode on ahead, his eyes darting about as he looked for the Weather Worker.

'Amira, this stone you showed Professor Dias. You said it was smooth. What did it look like?' asked Gem.

'It was so pretty,' she said. 'It was almost perfectly round, and once I'd polished the dust off, it was the most gorgeous azure shade of blue!'

Gem's cheeks flushed with colour. Without saying a word she turned and chased after the others. Renzo and Mr Donatello were standing on a rock, gazing around. Mrs Silva was peering past the trees.

'Are you all right, Gem?' asked Renzo, noticing her bright eyes.

'I'm not sure I can explain just yet,' the little witch said, her voice high with excitement. 'It couldn't possibly be true – yet perhaps it is. You see, I'm certain the Weather Worker is on this island, and I believe I know why!'

For a few seconds there was total silence. Then there was a loud CRASH. Thunder clapped overhead. The sky thickened with yellow cloud. The calm, cloudy weather had simply been the eye of the storm: the worst of it was about to arrive!

'What do you mean?' cried Mrs Silva. 'Where is he? What's happened to him?'

Gem pulled out the ripped page from the Weather Worker's diary from her pocket. It was only a scrap, but it was enough. 'Nothing has happened to him. In fact, you could say that he's the one doing something!'

She held the torn page up above her head and chanted the returning spell. Everyone watched the piece of paper rise up and speed towards the northern edge of the island.

'Come on,' she said, being sure to keep her voice quiet. 'Let's go!'

Over many years, the sea wind had blown at the trees so that they were bent and twisted and low to the ground. The group had to climb under gnarled branches, over rocks and through thick bracken to reach the northern point.

At the same time, the vicious storm brewed above them. The rain began to fall harder and faster, and the wind blew and blew, sending terns dashing to their nests. Tree branches lashed against their faces and they could hear huge waves exploding over the rocks. Thunder burst overhead and lightning lit up the sky, but the group kept going.

Soon Little Gem could smell something burning.

The trees began to thin and the sea, surging with foam, became visible again.

Suddenly, they all stopped. They'd come to a steep drop over the rocks, leading down to the beach. Even through the rain the smell of smoke was stronger than ever.

‘There’s nothing here,’ said Amira. Her wet headscarf draped against her cheeks and she shivered miserably.

‘I suppose the spell was wrong,’ said Mrs Silva, panting. ‘Never mind. We should get to shelter before we’re hit by lightning!’

But then they all noticed Professor Dias’ boat dragged up onto the far end of the stony beach.

Before anyone could stop her, Gem was clambering down the rock face. It was about five times her height. Several times she nearly slipped, but she held on and made it to the bottom.

And there she found a secret cave.

Chapter Twenty-seven

The cave was dark and smoky. There was a waterproof sheet hung across the entrance, which had been pulled back to let in the light. Inside, she could see a small camp bed, several large water bottles and a pile of tinned food. In the centre of the cave a dirty man with a stubbly chin was sitting on a camping stool, his back to them.

It was the Weather Worker!

He turned and jumped with fright.

'A witch!' he said. 'What are you doing here –'

'You wretch!' interrupted Mrs Silva, appearing behind Gem. Her nose was pink with cold. 'You birdbrain! You absolute nincompoop!' She hugged her brother and then stamped her foot.

'How dare you – I'm *so* cross – I could kill you – are you all right?'

Then Amira appeared. 'What are you doing here, Professor Dias?' Amira asked. 'When was the last time you showered?'

Mr Dias looked confused.

'What are you all doing here? How did you find me?'

Everyone started speaking at once, but Gem's voice cut through the chatter. 'I see what's going on here,' she said with confidence.

The group stopped and looked her way. Outside, the storm grew fiercer and the weatherproof sheet flapped loudly in the wind. She had to raise her voice to be heard.

'Amira found a stone,' she said slowly. 'She found a special stone, and she brought it to Professor Dias last Wednesday, so that they could identify it together.'

'Right so far,' said the Weather Worker. His eyes were red and puffy.

'I think Professor Dias realised that this was not just any stone,' Gem went on. 'In fact, he realised that this was not a stone at all. He realised that Amira had found an egg – a dragon egg.'

Henry turned completely invisible. Everyone gasped, and Amira leant against the cave wall in shock. 'I found a dragon egg?' she said. 'It can't be true!'

But Professor Dias nodded. 'Precisely,' he said. 'You're very clever.'

'So last Wednesday,' said Gem, 'Professor Dias was eating his lunch and trying to identify the stone. When he realised it was a dragon egg, he got so excited that he ran into town, borrowed

Renzo's camping equipment and came straight here to try to hatch it.'

'Why didn't you tell me!' Mrs Silva wailed. 'I was so worried – you big buffoon – you cracker-head!'

'I did tell you!' Professor Dias was indignant. 'I wrote you a note!'

'A note . . .?' Mrs Silva said. 'You sent me a scrap of paper that said "special tip orange replacement", if I remember correctly. It didn't make any sense!'

'Silly Sara – it said "special trip, arrange replacement".' Professor Dias threw his arms in the air. 'So that's why the weather is mad! I thought someone was in charge this whole time.'

'Dragons are connected to the weather,'

Henry interjected thoughtfully. 'Rain, specifically, and typhoons. I remember from when I was alive.'

'Who's speaking? Is that – why, you must be Ghost Henry!' The Weather Worker looked thoroughly stunned. 'Well, I'll come back immediately. This has been a great failure, anyway.'

They all gathered around the camping stove. The egg was about the size of a grapefruit, and it shone in the light.

'It's been seven days and six nights,' said Professor Dias. 'I've managed to keep the fire going even with this terrible weather. I haven't slept in days. But it's all for nothing. The egg hasn't hatched. Perhaps I should have used a wood fire. Or perhaps the egg is too old. But no matter. I give up.' He sat down heavily in the camping chair. 'It simply isn't going to work.'

'Good,' said Henry, reappearing, 'because dragons are horrible!'

'They're an extinct species,' retorted the Weather Worker, 'a valuable part of nature. It would be a scientific miracle!'

But Gem wasn't listening to either of them. She crept right up close to the egg and smiled.

'I can help,' she said. 'I'm sure I know a spell for that.'

Chapter Twenty-eight

'On the last day of hatching, all the dragon mothers gather around the egg and blow fire upon it,' Gem said.

She began to chant a heating spell. The entire cave became hot. Gem brought her hands closer to the camping stove. Flames danced around the blue egg, which glittered like a crystal.

'They need a lot of heat for the shell

to crack,' Gem explained. 'It's the last burst of heat that really does it.'

The cave got hotter and smokier. Everyone was red-faced and sweaty.

'My clothes are drying,' said Renzo happily.

'It simply won't work,' said Professor Dias, fanning himself with his hat. 'It's very kind of you to try, but –'

There was a quiet *tap*.

Everybody knelt down in front of the camping stove and stared at the egg in wonder as a single crack appeared in the shell.

'Oh my goodness,' said Mr Donatello, running his fingers through his hair. 'I feel like I'm in a dream. This can't be happening!'

There was another sharp *tap* and a triangle of shell broke off. A scaly golden head peeked out, yawned, and then squeaked.

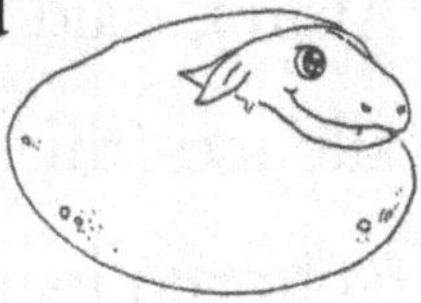

Everyone watched in awe as the tiny dragon shook itself out of the shell and flapped clumsily to the ground. The shell pieces fizzled and disappeared in the flames.

A real dragon!

The creature was the size of a small lizard. It had a long, spiky tail and green eyes that glittered in the light. It squeaked again, rolled over and examined each of them in turn.

Then it crept forward and rested its

head on Amira's foot, gazing up at her lovingly.

'Amira,' said Professor Dias, breaking the silence, 'this little creature seems to have chosen its mother.'

Amira looked shocked. 'Me?' she said. 'I can't – I can't take care of a dragon! What will my parents say? What does a dragon even eat? I . . .'

But the dragon had chosen. It clawed up her woollen jumper and curled around her neck, purring like a cat.

By the time they'd packed up the cave, the worst of the storm had passed. The wind faded from a howl to a whisper. The rain fell only lightly. Broken tree branches were scattered across the beach and the boat was full of sand.

'You must be right about dragons and rain, Ghost Henry,' said Professor Dias, examining the sky. 'But I should have been there to manage the weather. I'm sorry, everybody.'

Chapter Twenty-nine

As they sailed back to Ellsworth Pining a waxing crescent moon glimmered dimly through the cloud. Amira had got over her shock and was now cuddling the dragon against her chest. It chirped happily as she scratched its belly.

'I'm going to call her Emerald,' said Amira, 'because she's precious – just like you, Little Gem!'

Gem smiled widely. She glanced at Henry, sitting beside her. She – the worst witch at Witchcraft School – had solved a mystery and hatched a dragon. Perhaps she was a good witch after all!

'Emilio, why didn't you tell us you were going to hatch a dragon?' asked Mr Donatello. 'We could have helped you. Instead we were worried sick!'

'I was so excited about the egg that I didn't think,' Professor Dias replied, half asleep. His beanie hat was saturated with rain. 'And I thought you might be angry. Dragons can be dangerous.'

'I'm certainly angry now.' Mrs Silva slapped him playfully across the arm.

'I was so distressed! We thought you'd been eaten by a ferocious beast!'

'A beast?' It was the Weather Worker's turn to look shocked, and everyone laughed.

'That's another story,' said Renzo, winking at Gem. 'We'll tell you later.'

When they pulled up at the pier, Professor Dias hurried back to his lighthouse.

'Thank you, Little Gem,' said Amira sincerely, stroking the dragon around her neck. Emerald chirruped cheerfully and licked her chin.

'Now our tiny town has a marvellous witch – and a dragon!' said Mrs Silva.

'It's really true, what they say – when a witch arrives in town, something mysterious is about to happen!'

Gem's cheeks hurt from smiling. 'I'm happy to be here,' she said. 'Thank you for your kindness.'

'We're lucky to have you,' said Renzo. And they all waved goodbye as Gem and Henry began the long walk home to Witch Cottage.

Gem didn't realise how exhausted she was until she got inside. She sank into her armchair, yawning. Pomelo leapt into her lap and rubbed his head against her chin.

'You did it, Gem!' said Henry, putting on a pot of tea. 'You solved the mystery!'

'*We* solved the mystery,' said Gem, but instead of feeling happy she felt worried. What would happen now? Witchcraft School felt like a bad dream. When she thought about those cold, damp halls, the inkpots and the frogs beneath her pillow, she shivered and held Pomelo tightly. She was happy in Ellsworth Pining, and did not want to leave her friends behind forever – especially not Henry.

'You know,' said Henry, arranging some biscuits on a plate, 'it would probably be a very bad idea for you to try to go back to school just yet. Sometimes your spells go wrong – you didn't send yourself to Ellsworth Pining on purpose,

you were only trying to get to the next classroom! What if you sent yourself to the moon? Or hundreds of years into the future? It would be downright dangerous!'

'You really think so?' said Gem hopefully.

'I know so.' Henry placed the tea and biscuits on the table. 'I think you'd better stay here a while longer, Witch Gem, and practise your magic.'

'And maybe,' said Gem, her heart brimming with happiness, 'we can solve a few more mysteries along the way!'

Acknowledgements

This book started out as a zine in 2014. Thank you to those who bought it, and to Sean, who encouraged me to make it in the first place.

Little Gem exists thanks to my parents – I was shaped by the books you shared with me. I could not have done this without your support. Dad, you are my co-author. Everything good in this book is indebted to you (except the pictures).

Thank you to my life models, Sean, J'etaime, Bonnie, Emmy and Phoebe.

Thanks so much to Zoe and Mary at Penguin Random House, who believed in me before I believed in myself.

And lastly, this is for you, 4C! You were the best and most hilarious class a graduate teacher could wish for (Rally? Volley? Relay . . .?). Miss Z, you developed the character Amira. Your advice, recommendations and styling solutions have been indispensable. Thank you for bringing her to life.

About the Author

Anna Zobel lives in Melbourne's west with her partner and their chatty cat Harriet. When she's not writing or illustrating, Anna enjoys a variety of stimulating hobbies including reading, gardening, and eating. She is inspired by the children she has encountered as a babysitter, after-school care assistant and teacher, and strives to represent them in her work.

ANNA ZOBEL
Little Gem
and the Mysterious Letters

Read on for a sneak peek of

Little Gem and the Mysterious Letters

Chapter One

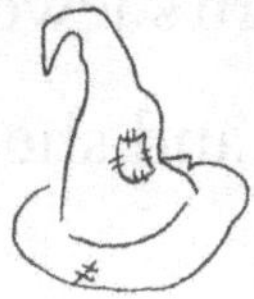

The summer sun shone brightly through the window of Witch Cottage. Sitting at the kitchen table were Gem, Ghost Henry and their friend Amira. Amira was holding a baby dragon tightly between her hands.

'You say she ate an earring?' said Witch Gem, peering inside the dragon's mouth with a small torch.

'Seven earrings,' said Amira, sounding

worried. 'Silly Emerald! She got into my mum's jewellery box while we were asleep, and she hasn't stopped hiccuping since.'

Emerald inhaled.

'*Move!*' said Henry quickly, and Gem ducked out of the way as another hiccup erupted from the dragon. A small ball of flame shot across the room and hit the bookshelf. Henry chased it with a damp towel.

Gem turned back to her book. She'd learnt about dragons at Witchcraft School, but there was still a lot she didn't know. 'There's nothing in here about what to do when a dragon eats earrings,' she said thoughtfully, turning the pages.

'There's a whole chapter on diet, of course – we read that carefully straight after she hatched –'

'Insects. Mice. Bones to keep her teeth clean,' recited Amira. 'No tomatoes. No grapes. Absolutely *no* apricots.'

'And there's the chapter on common dragon illnesses –' Gem went on.

'Claw rot. Gummy ear. Belly bloat. Metabolic smoke disease,' said Amira, stroking Emerald's tiny wings.

'But nothing about earrings.' Gem peered inside Emerald's mouth again, squinting.

'I say we try the pickled koria root,' said Ghost Henry. 'A classic remedy for animal poisonings. Remember when Mr Tiatia's goat ate all that pokeweed? It worked like a charm!'

Gem sighed. 'Goats and dragons are so different … but I think you're right, Henry. It won't do any harm, anyway –'

'*Move!*' yelled Amira.

But it was too late.

Emerald hiccuped loudly, and an orange ball of flame shot out and caught Gem's long, tangled hair.

But Henry had a bucket ready – they always kept a bucket ready when Emerald came over – and in a matter of seconds he'd tipped the cold water over Gem's head.

She stood still, dripping, as tendrils of pale smoke curled upwards from her hair towards the ceiling.

'Sorry,' said Amira.

The tiny golden dragon gave an apologetic cheep.

'Not to worry,' said Gem, blinking away the droplets that clung to her eyelashes. 'It isn't the first time.' She wiped her face dry on the hem of her dress and turned to fetch a jar from the shelf, her shoes squeaking noisily against the wet flagstones. Twisting the lid off the jar, she pulled out what looked like a purple pickled onion.

'Thank goodness she's not a fussy eater,' said Gem, feeding the koria root to Emerald.

They all watched carefully as the sick dragon chewed and swallowed. She licked her lips and blinked, her green eyes glinting in the light. Then she froze – her scaly face paled – she took a deep breath, and . . .

SPLASH!

The table was splattered with purple dragon spit. All three of them leant forward for a closer look.

'*Eight* earrings,' said Henry, poking the mess with a fork, 'and a pencil sharpener.'

'It smells a bit like rockmelon,' said Gem with a careful sniff.

Amira pulled out what looked like a long, sticky piece of string. 'My rainbow shoelace,' she said. 'I've been looking for this everywhere!'

Emerald, clearly feeling better, chirruped cheerfully and flew up to Amira's shoulder.

Gem gave the objects a rinse in the old stone sink. She smiled to herself, gazing out the window towards the pine forest. There was no better feeling than helping a friend. Gem loved to help, and with practice and experience her magic was improving every day.

'We should bottle this dragon spit, Gem,' said Henry, interrupting her thoughts. 'I don't remember what it does, exactly, but I think it has healing powers.'

Gem passed a small glass bottle to Henry, who began to fill it up with purple goop. Then she dried off the objects and returned them to Amira.

'Thanks so much, you two,' said Amira gratefully. 'Looking after Emerald is hard work. Nobody around here has any idea what to do with a dragon, not even Mr Dias or the town vet!'

'We know a little,' said Gem, 'but we're learning too.'

'Well, thanks again,' said Amira. 'I'm going straight to the hall. Are you coming?'

'We'll meet you there,' said Gem. 'I just have a few more things to do.'

This busy witch had letters to open and potions to make!